HORROR COLLECTOR

1 The Faceless Kid

Midori Sato and Norio Tsuruta

Illustration by
Yon

New York

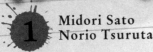

1

Midori Sato
Norio Tsuruta

Translation by Jan Cash
Cover art by Yon

This book is a work of fiction. Names, characters, places, and incidents are the product of the author's imagination or are used fictitiously. Any resemblance to actual events, locales, or persons, living or dead, is coincidental.

KYOFU COLLECTOR Vol.1 KAO NO NAI KODOMO
©Midori Sato/Norio Tsuruta 2015
©Yon 2015
First published in Japan in 2015 by KADOKAWA CORPORATION, Tokyo.
English translation rights arranged with KADOKAWA CORPORATION, Tokyo
through TUTTLE-MORI AGENCY, INC., Tokyo.

English translation © 2023 by Yen Press, LLC

JY
150 West 30th Street, 19th Floor
New York, NY 10001

Visit us at jyforkids.com • facebook.com/jyforkids • twitter.com/jyforkids
jyforkids-blog.tumblr.com • instagram.com/jyforkids.com

First JY Edition: November 2023
Edited by Yen On Editorial: Leilah Labossiere
Designed by Yen Press Design: Wendy Chan

JY is an imprint of Yen Press, LLC.
The JY name and logo are trademarks of Yen Press, LLC.

The publisher is not responsible for websites (or their content) that are not owned by the publisher.

Library of Congress Cataloging-in-Publication Data
Names: Sato, Midori, 1977– author. | Yon, illustrator. | Tsuruta, Norio,
    1960– editor. | Cash, Jan Mitsuko, translator.
Title: Horror collector / Midori Sato ; illustration by Yon ; editorial
    supervision by Norio Tsuruta ; translated by Jan Cash.
Other titles: Kyofu collector. English
Description: First JY edition. | New York, NY : Yen On, 2023– | Contents:
    v. 1. The faceless kid — | Audience: Ages 8–12 | Audience: Grades 4–6 |
Identifiers: LCCN 2023031049 | ISBN 9781975378226 (v. 1 ; trade paperback) | ISBN 9781975378240
    (v. 2 ; trade paperback) | ISBN 9781975378264 (v. 3 ; trade paperback) | ISBN 9781975378288 (v. 4 ; trade
    paperback) | ISBN 9781975378301 (v. 5 ; trade paperback) | ISBN 9781975378325 (v. 6 ; trade paperback)
Subjects: LCGFT: Horror fiction. | Light novels.
Classification: LCC PZ7.1.S26498 Ho 2023 | DDC [Fic]—dc23
LC record available at https://lccn.loc.gov/2023031049

ISBNs: 978-1-9753-7822-6 (paperback)
        978-1-9753-7823-3 (ebook)

10 9 8 7 6 5 4 3 2 1

LBK

Printed in the United States of America

HORROR COLLECTOR

1 The Faceless Kid

Shiori

Hey, I have a question

6:30 PM

Miku

Read
6:31 PM
What?

Shiori

Do you think it's true that if you
meet a hooded kid from out of town,
weird things will happen to you?

6:31 PM

Miku

Read
6:32 PM
Oh yeah, I know that rumor

Shiori

Some people say the kid
is wearing a red hood, but
others say it's actually black

6:32 PM

Miku

Read
6:33 PM
That's what I've heard, too

Shiori

And some people say the kid is a boy,
but others say they're a girl, right?

6:34 PM

Miku

Read
6:34 PM
Yeah, supposedly

CONTENTS

The Wriggler

It's white and human shaped and writhes when it moves. Supposedly, if you see it up close, something terrible will happen to you. The internet has plenty of theories about it—some people claim it's a ghost, while others say it's just a mirage—but nobody actually knows much about it. Most people have seen it near water.

"So have you heard about the faceless kid?"

They were on their way home.

When Natsuna Aikawa glanced at Yurie Miyamoto, who was walking ahead of her, she looked fed up.

Natsuna hated two things: One was picking up bugs, and the other was listening to her sixth-grade classmate Yurie talk about urban legends. On the other hand, Yurie's favorite pastime was searching for new spooky stories online, and she especially loved to regale Natsuna and their other best friend, Rin Oomori, with her frightening finds during their walk from school.

Some urban legends Natsuna and Rin had already been subjected to included the dog with the human face and toilet-bound Hanako, but no matter how many stories she heard, Natsuna always shuddered with every new one, and she wasn't interested in hearing more.

Unfortunately, Yurie loved scaring her friends, so whenever she discovered a terror from the internet's treasure troves, she had to give them all the info.

It seemed that day's new gem was the faceless kid.

"It's super popular on the internet lately. If you meet a kid wearing a hood, they say weird things will start happening around you."

"Weird things? Like what?" Natsuna asked. Yurie responded with "Hmm."

"I dunno what that means exactly, but anyway, weird things happen. There's lots of online posts from people who've seen the kid. Some say they're wearing a red hood; others say it's black; sometimes they're a girl, and others, a boy."

"Well, I guess that one's a little interesting..."

Natsuna thought right then that it was the vaguest urban legend she'd heard so far. It wasn't scary—just a head-scratcher—but that also meant she might get through the day without feeling goose bumps all over. But Natsuna didn't get to bask in her relief for too long. Yurie grinned as though she'd picked up on those feelings.

"But here's the part that makes it scary—" Yurie suddenly became serious as she gave Natsuna and Rin a pointed look.

Natsuna couldn't help but gulp nervously.

"So somebody's curiosity got the better of them, and they looked at the kid's face under the hood," Yurie continued. "And the kid didn't have eyes, a nose, or a mouth!"

"Like, nothing at all?"

Their face was just smooth? So that's why they're the faceless kid? Natsuna's whole body shuddered at the thought.

It looked like today's story actually *was* creepy, too.

Then Rin, who hadn't said a word until then, stared directly at Yurie and said, "Are you sure that's not all made up?"

Rin liked urban legends just about as much as Natsuna. However, unlike Natsuna, instead of feeling creeped out, she looked angry.

"Yurie, those stories sound like they're full of baloney. There's no such thing as a kid without a face."

Natsuna nodded along with Rin, but Yurie seemed unconvinced. She glared at Rin, looking serious.

"If it's all fake, then explain why people say they've actually seen the kid."

Unlike Rin, Yurie really believed in the legends, and that was why she hunted them down every day on the internet.

"There are tons of witnesses who've posted online about all the real urban legends they've *actually* come across. Are you saying they're all liars?"

"Well…"

Rin suddenly had no idea what to say. She really didn't think *everyone* was making up their stories. That was when Natsuna turned to her two friends as if she'd just thought of something.

"But I've never heard of it happening to anyone I know personally." Not a single one of her friends or her family members had ever come across a real-life urban legend. "You've never seen one for real either, right, Yurie?"

"I haven't, but…" Yurie deflated as she replied to Natsuna.

When Rin saw that, it was her turn to give Yurie a sharp glare.

"So you really don't know whether any of it is true, then."

"Well…I guess not."

"So that means all of it could be made up?"

"Yeah…" Yurie didn't have any other answer. She hung her head and looked at the ground.

"Yurie…" Natsuna felt kind of bad, so she broke in between the two. "Rin, that's enough about this for today."

"But—," Rin started to say.

"I know urban legends are scary, but Yurie just likes them, okay? And we're all friends, aren't we?"

Once Natsuna said that, Rin answered, "Okay, fine… Sorry, Yurie. We went too far."

"No, actually, I'm sorry for scaring you all the time with my stories."

Yurie bobbed her head at Rin in apology. It seemed as though she'd reflected on what she'd done. Rin smiled and seemed in a better mood after that, too.

"Okay, let's all go home, then!" Natsuna said brightly, and started walking off with her two friends.

"What's that?"

After taking five steps, Natsuna suddenly heard Yurie whisper to her from behind.

"What's wrong?"

Natsuna turned around to see that Yurie wasn't fooling around. She was staring at a rice paddy by the roadside.

"Over there..." Yurie pointed at the center of the field.

Natsuna and Rin, still puzzled, looked in that direction.

"Uh?"

They saw something in the field that was white and vaguely human shaped.

"What is that thing?"

It was four PM in mid-July, so it was a bright day, and they had a clear view of the thickly growing rice paddies. But for some reason, the white thing wasn't in focus at all. It looked almost like a shadow. Its face, body, arms, and legs were just white outlines, and its whole entire body wiggled weirdly while it stood right in the center of the rice field.

"Is someone playing a prank on us?" Natsuna murmured with fear. "But how did they make themselves look like that?"

Maybe the person was wearing a full bodysuit? Or maybe they were using smoke to make themselves look hazy?

Natsuna tried to think of an explanation, when suddenly she heard something deep in her head.

Riiing.

It was a high-pitched metallic sound.

"Ahhh…"

When Natsuna heard the ringing in her head, she felt pain, too—and this wasn't just any regular old headache, either. It felt as if someone were pounding on her skull from the inside.

"Oww!" It hurt so much, Natsuna could only hold her head.

"Yurie, Rin, help!" she cried out.

Natsuna looked over at her two friends, but they were clutching their heads just like she was.

"Natsuna! My head, it's—"

"Mine too…"

"Yurie… Rin…"

Riiing. Riiing.

The sharp metallic sound was even louder than before.

Natsuna started to panic. It hurt so much, she was afraid her head would split.

"Let's go home!" Natsuna said, and Yurie and Rin both eagerly nodded.

All three of them sprinted away.

After a while, Natsuna and her friends stopped running. For some reason, the pain in their heads had disappeared, and they couldn't hear the ringing anymore, either.

"What happened?"

"It doesn't hurt anymore…"

"Same…"

They felt fine now.

They'd sprinted for three minutes straight, trying to get distance from the field.

"What just happened?"

The three girls tilted their heads, trying to figure it out. They had no idea what caused the headaches in the first place or what had made them feel better. Either way, they all were afraid the terrible pain would come back, and they hurried home.

The next day.

Natsuna's head hadn't hurt even once since then. Other than feeling a little uneasy, she was in tip-top shape, so she went to school just like usual.

While she was walking, Natsuna suddenly remembered everything that had happened the day before.

What was that white thing?

She was passing by the rice paddy just then.

It might still be here…

Natsuna cautiously looked over at the field, but all she saw were plants—nobody was there.

I guess it really was someone playing a prank on us.

Still lost in thought, Natsuna kept walking toward school.

When she got to the classroom, Rin was already sitting in her seat.

"Good morning," Natsuna said, and Rin greeted her back, so Natsuna asked her, "Rin, how's your head?"

"It's fine. No pain since yesterday."

Natsuna felt relieved to hear that. She looked around the classroom and realized Yurie still wasn't there.

"Where's Yurie?"

"She's not here yet," Rin answered.

"Huh… That's not like her."

Yurie was usually at school before the two of them.

"Maybe her head started hurting again?" Natsuna said.

Rin gave her a worried look. "What? No way…"

Right then, the classroom door opened, and their home-room teacher, Mr. Aoyama, came in.

"Everyone, please don't panic, and listen to me carefully." Mr. Aoyama, who was normally smiling and cheerful, looked very serious. "Your classmate Yurie Miyamoto was in a traffic accident this morning."

"What?!" Natsuna's eyes went as wide as saucers.

"She was taken to a hospital, but she's still unconscious," Mr. Aoyama continued.

All the students started to talk at the same time:

"What?!"

"Yurie is in the hospital?!"

Meanwhile, Mr. Aoyama looked at Natsuna and Rin, who was sitting next to her.

"Natsuna Aikawa, Rin Oomori, you're very close with Yurie Miyamoto, aren't you?" he said.

"Yes, we're best friends," Natsuna answered.

"Then you might understand what she yelled right before the accident."

Mr. Aoyama stared at the two of them. The other kids also stopped chattering and looked at them, too.

"She was apparently running away from something on a road near her house," Mr. Aoyama said. "Then she ran into an intersection and was hit by a truck. When she ran into the road, she yelled, 'The *blank* is after me.'"

"The blank?"

Natsuna immediately thought of the white figure. Panicking, she looked at Rin, who seemed to have thought the same thing and was staring back at her. All the blood had drained from Rin's face.

"Do the two of you know anything about this?" Mr. Aoyama asked.

"Well… Um…"

Neither Natsuna nor Rin knew how to explain it, so they both stayed silent.

After school.

Natsuna and Rin were in the middle of a gloomy walk home. In the end, they hadn't been able to tell Mr. Aoyama about the white figure.

"He wouldn't believe us even if we told him."

"Yeah, I don't think he would…"

Rin and Natsuna were both terrified. The "blank" thing

Yurie had shouted about had to be the white figure they'd seen the other day. The more Natsuna thought about it, the more terrified she became.

"Hey, you two."

They heard a boy's voice come from behind them.

When Natsuna and Rin turned around, they saw a boy around their age standing alone in the road. He was dressed in red, and a red hood covered his head. Natsuna was taken aback when she saw that. He perfectly fit the description of an urban legend Yurie told them about the day before.

"The faceless kid wears a red hood..."

"There's no way...," Natsuna started to say.

But when she peered under his hood, she saw a boy with pale skin, large clear eyes, a straight nose, and thin, pretty lips. He was actually kind of handsome. At first, Natsuna felt relieved to see he was just a regular boy, but then she started to feel doubts as she wondered why he'd called out to them.

"Um, do you need something from us?" she asked.

"Yes, I do." The boy eyed Natsuna and Rin as he walked over to them. "You two are friends with Yurie Miyamoto, the girl who was in an accident, aren't you?"

"Huh?! Do you know Yurie?" Natsuna asked, but the boy shook his head.

"I don't know her, but I do know about the *being* that was following her."

"The *being*?" Natsuna looked puzzled by the boy's phrasing.

Rin was also stunned, and her eyes widened.

As he observed them, the boy said, "Did your heads suddenly hurt after you saw something yesterday?"

"After we saw something?" Natsuna was suddenly startled. "That did happen! Right after the three of us saw the white figure!"

Now that he'd mentioned it, they'd felt the head-splitting pain right when the white figure had appeared.

"I thought so…"

The boy nodded slightly as though he'd come to some sort of conclusion, then stared intently at Natsuna and Rin.

"I think the thing following her was a monster from urban legends called the wriggler."

"The wriggler…"

Natsuna and Rin had never heard of it before.

"It's usually seen in fields moving just like how it's named. And when anyone sees it, they suddenly hear metal clanging and get a headache. But you absolutely shouldn't ever look at it. If you do, the wriggler will follow you and you'll suffer a terrible fate."

"A terrible fate…?"

"That's right, and it has another name: the Blank," the boy said.

"That's it!" Natsuna exclaimed.

When Yurie was in the accident, she'd also shouted about something "blank."

"Then that's what happened to Yurie?!"

Natsuna was suddenly filled with fear. Yurie had been chased by the wriggler and ended up in an accident. Natsuna was frightened, and even Rin started to tremble as she grabbed Natsuna's arm. It seemed like Rin was just as scared as she was.

But it turned out Rin was worried about something different.

"If it was chasing Yurie…," Rin said, "does that mean it'll go after us next?"

"What?" Natsuna said.

"Since we both saw the wriggler, too," Rin added, which startled Natsuna.

Rin was right. Yurie wouldn't be the only one the wriggler was after.

Natsuna looked Rin in the face and couldn't help but feel anxious. At this rate, they would both be attacked by the

wriggler like Yurie and something terrible would happen to them.

"What do we do now? Tell me!" Starting to panic, Natsuna turned back to the boy to beg for help.

But he wasn't there.

The moment Natsuna and Rin had taken their eyes off him, he'd disappeared.

"Natsuna, where did that boy go?" Rin asked.

"I'm not sure, but he was right there a second ago…"

The two girls could only stand there, dumbfounded.

That evening.

When Natsuna arrived home, she didn't eat dinner, just locked herself in her room. That worried her mom, who knocked on her door.

"Natsuna, what's wrong? Are you feeling sick?" her mom called in.

But Natsuna stayed curled up on her bed without responding.

What do I do? At this rate, the wriggler will catch up with me and Rin, too…

Her mom probably wouldn't believe her, especially not the part about the urban legend.

Natsuna had no idea what to do and just shivered in fear all alone.

Buzz, buzz.

Her phone vibrated on the table. She had a message from Rin.
Natsuna scrambled to read it.

Rin: I figured out a way to avoid whatever happens after seeing the wriggler.

How?!
Natsuna sent a message back and received a reply from Rin right away.

Rin: Come to the shrine on the hill. I'll show you there.

"The shrine on the hill?"
Natsuna had no idea why Rin would ask to meet her there, but she decided to head over immediately.

It was past eight PM.
Natsuna was in front of the shrine behind the school.

The shrine was on top of a hill and about thirty steps up some stone stairs. At the moment, Natsuna was standing on the lowest step.

The kids at the school called it the "hill shrine" and would play there a lot, but at night it wasn't lit, so no one approached it after sunset.

The sun had already set, and the shrine was dark.

It's a little scary…

Natsuna's entire body shuddered.

Rin had messaged her that there were two rules they needed to follow to make sure they didn't suffer a terrible fate. The first was to not tell anyone Natsuna was going to the shrine, and the other was to leave her cell phone at home. Natsuna had no clue why she needed to do either of these things, but Rin hadn't explained anything else.

Because of that, for reasons she didn't understand at all, Natsuna didn't let anyone know she was going to the shrine and left her phone at home.

I need Rin to tell me how to avoid whatever is going to happen, and fast!

Even though she was frightened, Natsuna started climbing the steps.

At the top of the stairs, a path led to the shrine's small entrance where the offering box was set. The rest of the area was surrounded by trees. Once Natsuna reached the top, she started to walk around the front of the shrine, searching for any sign of Rin.

At this time of night, no one else was around.

Where is Rin…?

Even though they were supposed to meet at the shrine, Rin hadn't told her exactly where. She couldn't call Rin even if she wanted to, since her phone was at home.

What do I do?

Natsuna felt uneasy and scared as she looked out for Rin.

"What's wrong?" Suddenly, she heard a man's voice from off to the side.

When she looked over, she saw a man in a tracksuit sitting on a bench. Maybe he was taking a break from a walk?

He saw Natsuna, stood up, and smiled.

"Um, I was supposed to meet my friend here…," she said.

"A friend? Ah, if that's who you're looking for, there was a girl behind the shrine," the man said.

"Oh, that's probably her! Thank you so much!"

After thanking the man, Natsuna ran behind the shrine.

Once she got there, she saw someone standing alone.

"Rin!" Natsuna called to her while running over, and the person turned to look back at her.

"Natsuna!"

It was Rin, just as she'd thought. When Natsuna got close enough to see Rin clearly, she breathed a sigh of relief.

"I was looking for you," she said.

"Sorry. I didn't tell you exactly where to go."

"So how do we make sure that nothing bad will happen to us even though we've seen the wriggler?"

Natsuna had come all the way here to ask that.

"Someone told me he would explain how," Rin said.

"Someone? Do you mean the boy in the red hood?"

He had told them about the wriggler. Had Rin met him again after that?

But then Rin shook her head.

"It wasn't him. But another person knew about the wriggler."

"Then who was it?"

Natsuna was doubtful there really was a person like that.

Rustle, rustle!

Suddenly, they heard the trees moving behind them. At the same time, Natsuna felt a dull pain in her head.

"Ah!"

When she turned around, Natsuna saw Rin's face twisted in fear, then a white figure, but then she lost consciousness.

When Natsuna woke, she saw a pure-white ceiling. She felt like something was wrong and touched her head, only to find it was bandaged.

Natsuna was apparently lying on a hospital bed.

"What's…going on?"

When she turned to the side, she saw Rin sitting in a chair with a bandage also wrapped around her head. Rin was looking down and crying.

"Rin…," Natsuna called out to her, and her friend quickly lifted her head.

"Natsuna! You're awake?!" She smiled and hugged Natsuna. "Thank goodness!"

"Rin, why am I in the hospital?" Natsuna asked with a tilt of her head, and the smile suddenly disappeared from Rin's face.

"I'm sorry. It's all my fault…," Rin said, and she started to tell her what had happened.

Natsuna and Rin had apparently been attacked by a man.

"A man?"

"Yeah, a stranger. He was trying to kidnap us."

According to Rin, the man had overheard their conversation with the boy in the red hood. Then he'd taken advantage of what they'd talked about and told Rin he knew a way to escape the wriggler and to call Natsuna to the shrine. He'd also told them not to tell anyone or to bring their phones to make it easier to kidnap them.

"The police caught him earlier, though. They said you spoke to him, too."

"That man might have been…"

It had to have been the man who told her where to find Rin at the shrine. The white figure Natsuna had seen out of the corner of her eye had probably been his white tracksuit.

"No one is usually at the shrine. Luckily, there was a boy there that day, and he told the police…"

Thanks to that, Natsuna and Rin had escaped with slight injuries.

"I'm sorry, Natsuna…" Rin sobbed and bowed her head.

"It's not your fault, Rin. So chin up."

But Natsuna couldn't feel upset at her. Rin had just been worried about the terrible fate that was waiting for them, and Natsuna understood exactly how she felt.

"It's fine, since we haven't been attacked by the actual Blank," Natsuna said with a smile, but right then, she thought of something.

Blank…

"Maybe the white thing following after us was…" Natsuna remembered what Yurie had said during the accident and turned to look at Rin. "Wait, Yurie was in an accident near her house, right?"

"Yeah, Mr. Aoyama said she was at an intersection really close by."

"Doesn't a dog named Blanc live near her?"

"Blanc? Oh, right!" Rin exclaimed.

One of the neighbors had a large white dog named Blanc. When Natsuna and Rin would go to Yurie's house to play, the dog would bark at them a lot.

"So Yurie was chased by Blanc!"

"You're right! That must be it!" Rin brightened up.

It wasn't Blank the monster, but Blanc the dog. The dog had probably gotten off its leash and chased Yurie into the intersection. In other words, she hadn't been chased by the wriggler at all.

"Thank goodness."

Natsuna and Rin suddenly felt relieved. They were still worried about Yurie, but nothing bad would happen to them.

"Oh, you're awake." A nurse had noticed them and peeked into the room. "You two came out of this very lucky that you weren't too badly hurt."

When the nurse said that, Natsuna and Rin both gave an enthusiastic "Uh-huh!"

"Oh, right, you two are friends with Yurie Miyamoto, aren't you? She just woke up, too."

"Huh?! Yurie's awake?!"

They were at the same hospital as Yurie.

"Rin, let's go see her!" Natsuna said.

"Okay!"

The two of them excitedly headed off to Yurie's room.

At the same time near the intersection where Yurie had been hit, the boy in the red hood was talking to the woman who owned Blanc.

"You think Blanc chased a girl?" she asked him.

"I just thought it might be a possibility," the boy said.

But the woman replied, "That's just not possible." She explained, "We keep Blanc tied up very firmly. And Blanc has never run away before or chased any kids."

The boy looked at Blanc, who was next to the front door. Just as she'd said, a cable was secured to Blanc to keep it near the house. The dog was barking, but it seemed to be doing that because it was afraid of people. It really didn't seem like the type of dog that would chase after anyone.

"I see… Thank you," the boy said to the woman.

Then the boy left.

"It looks like that dog really didn't have anything to do with it. That must mean 'Blank' is actually…"

Suddenly, the boy thought of something.

Meanwhile, Natsuna and Rin walked into Yurie's hospital room.

"Yurie!"

They found her sitting on the bed.

"Oh, good! I was so worried!"

Natsuna and Rin smiled and ran over to Yurie's side.

"Blanc the dog chased after you, right?"

"What a bad dog."

Natsuna and Rin both eagerly started talking to Yurie. However, she didn't say anything and only shivered.

"What's wrong, Yurie?"

"Does it hurt?"

When Yurie looked at them, the color had drained from her face.

"No…," she said.

"Huh? What do you mean?"

"I wasn't attacked by a dog…," Yurie told them.

"What?"

Right then, Yurie looked at the door. Natsuna and Rin both followed her gaze.

They saw someone in white.

But it wasn't a person—it was the monster from the urban legend creepily wriggling right in front of them…

The monster slowly started to approach the girls.

"No!" Natsuna grabbed a vase on a shelf near the bed and threw it at the being. "Yurie! Rin! We need to run!"

The two others reacted when Natsuna shouted. Yurie still struggled to walk, so Natsuna pulled her by the arm, and all three of them dodged the white figure as they bolted out of the room.

"Somebody help!" Natsuna yelled as she ran down the hall.

But right at the time when they needed someone most, the hallway was empty.

"Where is everybody?!" Natsuna shouted.

"Natsuna, we need to go downstairs! Everyone should be downstairs!" Yurie told her.

The reception desk was there, and usually, there was a whole crowd around.

"All right!" Natsuna replied, and started to head for the stairs.

Snatch!

Suddenly, Natsuna felt something slippery and gross on her arm. She spun around and found that the white figure was right in front of her and holding on to her arm.

"Aaaah!" Yurie and Rin both screamed.

The white figure wriggled and pulled Natsuna closer.

"No… No… Noooo!" Natsuna's voice echoed through the halls.

When they heard the commotion, the receptionist and nurses downstairs ran up.

"What's wrong?!" the nurse asked as she made it to the hallway.

But no one was there.

Natsuna, Rin, Yurie, and even the white figure had disappeared as if they'd gone up in smoke.

After that, the three girls were never heard from again.

An urban legend that's primarily been spread around the internet. There's a house where a red crayon lies abandoned and supposedly doesn't belong to anyone. And in that house, there's a hidden room where the walls have been covered with red writing that says, "LEt mOmMY OuT."

Second Town

The Truth of the Red Crayon

"Wooow, it's soooo big!"

When Madoka Shinohara saw the house, she couldn't help but shout.

Madoka was a fifth grader whose short chestnut-brown hair and large eyes were her trademarks.

It was early afternoon on a Sunday, and Madoka had just moved into a house with her family. Their new home stood all on its own without sharing any walls with neighbors. It also had a white wall, a garden lined with trees, and even an iron gate at its entrance. It was all unfamiliar to Madoka, who had lived in a condo until then.

"It's an old building, but the previous owners took good care of it, so it's nice inside," Madoka's dad told her as he pulled bags from the trunk of the car.

"You've got a nice, big room, too, Madoka," her mom also said while getting out from the passenger side.

"Can I go look?"

"Of course. Your room is the farthest one on the second floor."

"Got it!"

Once Madoka was inside, she ran up the stairs to the second floor, where she discovered two rooms. After she walked a bit down the hall, she found one more. This was probably the room at the end of the hall her mom had told her about.

Thrilled, she opened the door.

"Whoa!"

When she saw the room, she couldn't help but exclaim in surprise again. It was even bigger and nicer than her mom had made it seem.

The room was spacious, and instead of being a traditional Japanese style, it looked more Western. Her things had already been moved into the room, and even her familiar bed and desk were there waiting for her.

"So this is my room starting today!"

The window was gigantic and south facing, so bright sunshine spilled into the room and illuminated it. Madoka's old room only had a tiny window that looked out onto the condo building next door, so she'd never gotten any sun and had to turn on her lights even during the day.

She hadn't liked that room and always complained about it to her parents. It seemed as though that had all paid off, and they'd picked out a house with tons of natural light.

"I think I'm going to enjoy this room!"

She grinned—she was already fond of it.

"That's good, Madoka."

"Yurika!"

Madoka dashed over to her little sister, who had stopped in front of her door at some point. Yurika was cradling her precious teddy bear as she stared at her older sister.

"Do you like our new house, Yurika?"

"Uh-huh!" Yurika replied enthusiastically. "I love it. We're still going to be friends even while we're here, right?"

"Of course we will be!" A smile popped onto Madoka's face. "You're my adorable little sister, after all. We're gonna be besties, just like we've always been."

Yurika gave another energetic "Uh-huh!" in reply.

The next day.

Madoka started going to her new school. She was in the fifth grade and ended up in classroom number three. She wasn't sure she'd have friends after transferring, but those fears were put to rest even before lunch break started.

Hardly any kids ever transferred to the school, so all her classmates naturally gathered around her.

Madoka also really liked talking to people. Because of her

bright personality, she could even chat easily with people she'd never met before. Thanks to that, when she ate lunch, she was already fast friends with two of her classmates, Momoka and Ai.

"Hey, Madoka, do you like urban legends?"

After the three of them had pushed their seats together to eat, Momoka casually asked Madoka that question.

"Urban legends? Um, I don't *dislike* them. I don't know much about them, though."

"Oh, really?" Ai and Momoka both said simultaneously after Madoka replied.

"So, lately, urban legends have been all the rage around school. Do you know about the wriggler, Madoka?" Momoka asked.

Madoka didn't, so she answered honestly, "No."

"The wriggler is this white human-shaped thing that wiggles around in rice paddies. These three sixth graders in another town happened to come across it. If you see the wriggler, that means you'll get attacked. Supposedly, all those girls got attacked by the wriggler and were never heard from again."

"They were what?" Madoka stopped eating and stared at Momoka. "Is that really true?"

"I dunno, but one of my study hall friends knows someone who lives in that town and told her about it. Apparently, they also saw the faceless kid there."

"A kid without a face? Is that another urban legend?"

"That's right. The kid is supposed to be a little boy who wears a hood, but he hasn't got eyes, a nose, or a mouth. Apparently, if you see him, weird things will start happening to you. Those girls saw him, so that's why they saw the wriggler."

Madoka couldn't believe any of what Momoka was saying, but then she started to think maybe things like that really could happen...

"But none of that happened in this town, right?"

All this stuff with the wriggler and faceless kid had happened in some place she'd never been to. As long as they didn't appear where she was, she had nothing to be frightened of, but this time Ai spoke up.

"Yeah, the wriggler and faceless kid were somewhere else, but we've got our own urban legend here, too."

"What is it?"

Her curiosity got the better of her, and Madoka had to ask. Ai's expression became serious, and she scooched her face right up to Madoka's.

"So this one's called The Red Crayon, and it's about a certain cursed house in town. One day, a family moved in, and supposedly, they found a red crayon inside it. Nobody in the family had crayons, though, so they had no idea where it'd come from. Then later, on another day, they found a hidden room in the house, and they decided to check it out.

And you know what they found there? All the walls had this little kid's creepy writing all over them, and it said, 'Let Mommy out, let Mommy out, let Mommy out…' And all of it was written in red crayon."

Madoka felt a shiver go down her spine.

When Ai saw that her new friend was spooked, she snickered under her breath.

"Looks like you're kind of a scaredy-cat, Madoka. Nobody knows which house it was, though, and it might not even be true, so don't be so afraid."

"Yeah, urban legends are just stories people tell. Also, we should hurry up and finish eating."

Momoka was snickering, too, though.

"Y-you're right," Madoka said as she laughed nervously. She felt embarrassed as she realized she'd let the silly story frighten her a little too much.

Urban legends are just stories. None of that's going to happen to me, Madoka thought, and she started eating her lunch again.

But just days later, Madoka had a strange encounter of her own…

That night, Madoka had a hard time sleeping.

She was in bed with her eyes shut tight, but for some reason, her mind was wide awake.

I have school tomorrow, so I need to sleep soon...

But the more Madoka thought that, the less sleepy she felt. She opened her eyes to check what time it was.

Right then, she heard something.

Aaaahhh!

It was a girl's scream, and it had come from outside her room.

"What was that?!"

Madoka scrambled out of bed in surprise.

According to her clock, it was past two o'clock in the morning.

She strained her ears to listen, but the whole house was silent again, and she didn't hear the girl's voice a second time.

"What was that just now?"

Even though she was scared, she opened her door and peered into the hallway.

But no one was there, and it was pitch-black.

Madoka picked up the flashlight left in the hallway for emergencies and lit up her surroundings.

I don't see anyone here...

She tried shining the flashlight all over the hall, but she didn't see anything out of the ordinary.

Maybe I was half-asleep and imagined it?

Madoka stood alone in the hallway and tilted her head quizzically.

The next morning.

When Madoka came out of her room, Yurika was standing in the hall. She was wearing her usual red dress and tight teddy bear in her arms.

Maybe the scream last night was Yurika's?

Madoka asked her about it.

"So you heard them last night?"

When Madoka asked her sister that, Yurika shook her head.

"I was asleep the whole night," she answered.

"Gotcha…"

But Madoka was sure the scream she'd heard had come from a little girl, and Yurika was the only other little girl in their house.

When Madoka got downstairs, she asked her parents, who were already eating breakfast, about the sound. Neither of them had shouted, and they hadn't heard anything during the night.

"If it was really that loud, we would have woken up, too," her dad told her.

"That's right," her mother said. "You must have dreamed it. You were probably tired from your first day at a new school."

"I guess...," Madoka said. Even though she wasn't fully convinced, she still assumed that must have been it.

But then a few days passed...

...and Madoka had another strange encounter...

On that day, when Madoka came home from school, she decided to head up to her room on the second floor to put her bag down before going to the living room for a snack.

"Huh?"

As she was headed up the stairs, she found something on the ground right in front of the steps. She stared at it, wondering what it could be.

It was a red crayon.

It seemed well used and was already half gone.

"What's this doing here?"

Madoka picked up the crayon without thinking much of it and noticed that Yurika was peering down at her from the second-floor hallway.

"Hey, Yurika, is this your crayon?" Madoka looked up at her sister and asked, but Yurika just shook her head vigorously no.

"It's not mine," her little sister said.

"Oh, right. You don't draw."

Just in case, Madoka asked her mom, who was in the kitchen making dinner, but she didn't know where it had come from, either. Her dad, who was still at work, wouldn't use crayons.

"Then whose is it?"

Right at that moment, Madoka remembered the story Ai had told her.

"One day, a family moved in, and supposedly, they found a red crayon inside it."

"Wait, no way!"

Suddenly, Madoka was filled with fear and quickly threw the crayon into the living room garbage bin.

Ding-dong.

Their doorbell rang, and her mom yelled "Coming" as she went to answer it.

Then she returned right away.

"Madoka, your friend is here," her mom said.

"A friend? Is it Momoka? Or maybe Ai?"

"No, it's a boy. He's wearing a red hood."

"What?"

Who could it be? She didn't know any of the boys very well, so she doubted any of them would visit her at home.

"Wait, if he's wearing a red hood…"

She remembered what Momoka had said.

"The kid is supposed to be a little boy who wears a hood, but he hasn't got eyes, a nose, or a mouth."

"The faceless kid!"

Madoka poked her head around the door to get a peek at the entrance of the house before she'd even thought it through.

A boy wearing a red hood was standing there, just like her mom had said.

But this boy had eyes, a nose, and a mouth for sure.

"Madoka, is something wrong?" her mom asked from behind when she saw Madoka behaving oddly.

"Uh, no, n-nothing's wrong…" Madoka smiled awkwardly.

That's right. It's not like the faceless kid really exists…

If the boy hadn't had a face, her mom wouldn't have been acting normal when she came back inside the house. Besides, the faceless kid was just an urban legend—it was only a story people told.

Madoka felt silly for being so scared in the first place as she went to go greet the boy.

"Um, I'm Madoka. What's your name?" she asked.

The boy had pale skin, large and clear eyes, and a straight nose. Even his small lips were handsome. He seemed slightly older than Madoka. Even though he was hiding his face with his hood, he was surprisingly good-looking.

He stared at Madoka.

"I don't care about your name," he said. "I came here to warn you."

"Warn me?" Madoka had no idea what he meant by that.

But the boy didn't seem to care and just kept talking. "This house might be cursed by the red crayon—"

"What?" Madoka blurted out from shock. "How do you know about the red crayon?!"

She'd only found it ten minutes ago, but the boy already knew about it. As Madoka grew uncomfortable, the boy simply stared at her.

"I just know. But at this rate, you and your family are in danger of—"

Madoka felt a shudder go through her.

That was when her mom, who'd been listening the entire time from the living room, walked over to them.

"Excuse me! What are you telling my daughter?! Madoka, is this boy not one of your friends?"

"No, I've never met him…"

"Then I think it's about time you go home!" Madoka's mom seemed to be upset because she thought the boy was trying to scare Madoka.

"I'm telling you the truth," the boy said to her mom. He didn't show any sign of leaving, either.

"Leave! Go on, the sooner the better!" her mom shouted at the boy, and she ushered him out the door. "My word! I'm sure he must be a neighborhood troublemaker."

Madoka understood why her mom was bothered. Anyone would be if someone came by to tell them the house they'd just moved into was cursed. Madoka wanted to ask the boy questions, but it seemed she'd lost her chance.

But how did he know about the red crayon?

Madoka couldn't shake off that thought.

She'd only told Yurika and her mom about it, but then Madoka realized something.

Maybe he planted the red crayon here?

Her mom had said he must be a troublemaker, after all. In that case, maybe he'd left the crayon in their house to scare her family?

That's it! He was just playing a joke on us!

Madoka felt relieved as she went back to her room.

"Madoka…" When she got to the top of the stairs, Yurika

was standing in the hallway. "Did he say our house is cursed? I'm scared…"

It seemed Yurika had overheard them even from the second floor. She looked worried and was tightly clutching her teddy bear.

"Everything's okay. He was just playing a joke on us is all." Madoka gently ruffled Yurika's hair.

"Really?"

"Yeah, so you have nothing to worry about, okay?" Madoka said, then Yurika broke into a smile and answered, "Okay!"

That made Madoka smile back.

It was evening on the same day.

Madoka was reading comics late into the night in her room, so she wasn't asleep yet. It was already midnight.

She realized she needed to get to bed and quickly scrambled under the covers.

After a while, she started to nod off.

She was almost fully asleep.

—elp…

Suddenly, she heard a tiny whisper that seemed close to

fading away. At first, Madoka was convinced she'd dreamed it, but then the voice became clearer and clearer.

—elp me… —elp me… Help me!

Madoka's eyes snapped open.
Someone was calling for help.
She heard a loud clatter in the hallway.
Then she heard a young girl's voice.

Aaaahhh!

It was the same scream she'd heard before.
"I'm not dreaming!"
She wasn't half-asleep this time.
Madoka rushed into the hall.

The hall was lit slightly by the moonlight, so Madoka could peer down it as she searched for the owner of the voice.
But she didn't see anyone at all.
"How could that be…?"
Maybe she really had been half-asleep?
Right then, as Madoka was staring down the hallway, she realized something was on the ground next to the wall.

"Wait, is that…?" She got closer and discovered it was a bear stuffed animal that had been abandoned. "This is Yurika's…"

Madoka picked up the bear and couldn't help but think the worst.

"Was that scream Yurika's?!" The thought sent a jolt through her. "Yurika! Yurika!"

Madoka began shouting her sister's name, but no matter where she looked, she couldn't find her younger sister.

"Yurika! If you're here, answer me! Come on, Yurika!"

Then she heard a feeble voice come from somewhere.

Help… Help… Help me, Big Sis…

That was definitely Yurika's voice.

"Yurika, where are you?!"

Madoka started to search where she thought she'd heard the voice coming from.

"Oh!"

She realized that the wall at the very end of the hall was slightly offset. Looking closely, she found that one of the panels was loose and led to a hollow space.

"Was that noise from earlier the wall panel falling off?"

The opening was just wide enough for one person.

"Yurika, you're not in here, are you?!"

Madoka grabbed the flashlight in the hallway and quickly crouched into the opening.

When she crawled through on all fours, she realized the space was much bigger on the inside than she'd thought it would be.

It seemed to be a small storage room.

It was probably about half the size of Madoka's room, and she could even stand all the way up inside it. But why was it sealed up with boards? She couldn't think of a good reason for hiding a storage space like this.

As she wondered about that, Madoka used the flashlight to look around.

"Yurika, where are you? Yurika?"

The room was filled with dust and smelled like mold, but it was completely empty. She would have noticed Yurika right away if her sister had been here.

"Yurika, are you not here? Answer me!"

Madoka lit up the space, searching corner to corner with the flashlight. Then she found something on the ground by a wall.

It was a half-used red crayon.

"Wait, isn't that—?"

Madoka knew it was the very same crayon she'd thrown away.

Why is this here?!

Had Yurika picked it out of the trash?

"Yurika! Tell me, where are you?!"

Madoka suddenly felt scared. She pointed the flashlight all over the room as she kept shouting Yurika's name.

Right then, when she lit up the wall for a moment, she saw something.

"Ah!" Madoka cried out instinctively.

She'd seen a line as red as blood along the wall. But it wasn't just one red line—there were a lot more bright-red marks all over the wall.

"What is this…?"

Madoka was frightened, but she aimed the flashlight at it.

That was when she realized it wasn't blood but crayon marks.

"Wait, does that mean…?"

Madoka glanced at the red crayon lying on the floor. The many, many red lines all over the wall seemed as if they'd come from that crayon. Madoka pointed the flashlight at the wall again and studied the lines this time. They appeared to be forming some sort of shape.

She backed away slightly to light up the entire wall.

"Huh…?" When she saw the whole drawing, a small noise escaped her.

At the same time, a shiver traveled down her spine, and her entire body trembled in fear.

"What is this…?"

She realized the walls weren't covered in ordinary lines at all.

The lines made up a drawing of people—four bloodstained people.

The biggest one held a knife and was attacking the two smaller figures. Both the ones being attacked were blotted out in bright red. The smallest one of the four was on the ground and also covered in red like the other two.

"Wh-what is this? No… Nooo!!!"

Madoka was so frightened, she rushed right out of the room.

"Dad! Help!"

As soon as she was out, she ran to her parents' room.

"What's wrong, Madoka?"

Her mom and dad got up from bed and looked at her, wondering what was going on.

"I saw a horrible drawing in this small room! And I can't find Yurika!" Madoka told her parents all about what had happened.

They looked dubious as they stared at her.

"What are you talking about?"

"I'm telling you, there was a small room! And I don't know what happened to Yurika!"

When Madoka said that, her dad looked puzzled. "Who's Yurika?"

"What?"

"We don't have another daughter, sweetie."

At that moment, Madoka's eyes went wide, and all she could do was let out a long "Uuhhh…"

Madoka hadn't known a girl named Yurika until she'd moved into this house.

"Then who was she…?" Madoka said.

While Madoka stood there confused, her mom asked, "Madoka, what's that you've got in your hand?"

Madoka suddenly realized she was still holding the teddy bear Yurika had dropped.

"What?!"

At some point, the bear had become ragged and mangled. It was even covered in bright red, but this time, the color wasn't from the red crayon. It was blood.

The teddy bear had been dyed red with blood.

"Aaaahhh!!!"

Filled with terror, Madoka fainted on the spot.

A whole month had passed.

Madoka and her family had practically run from the house in their haste to move out.

Right around the same time, a rumor had started to spread around her elementary school. This rumor claimed there was a part to the story of the red crayon that few people knew.

About a decade ago, a thief had broken into a house and killed the family that lived inside. The mother, father, and their six-year-old oldest daughter had all been killed.

But oddly, no one had been able to find the youngest daughter, who was a preschooler, no matter where they looked. That little girl had loved drawing with crayons, and supposedly, she was still hiding in the house to this day. Those who witnessed her claimed to see her drawing the scene of her family's murder.

This story was called The Truth of the Red Crayon, and it became yet another urban legend to be passed around.

Not long after, someone sneaked into the house Madoka's family had abandoned.

It was the boy in the red hood.

The boy climbed up to the second floor of the house and walked over to the wall at the end of the hall.

The boards had been put up again to seal the small room that lay beyond, so the boy pried a board loose and entered the space. Once he was inside, he shone a flashlight all around the room, as though he was searching for something. Eventually, he found something in a corner and approached it.

A strange mark had been carved there.

"Found it…"

The boy inspected it, then pulled a bright-red notebook from his pocket. He opened it and held it over the mark.

Then he chanted a spell:

"ɹǝsolⱯɿ."

In the next moment, the mark glittered, inverted, and appeared on the open page of the notebook.

Meanwhile, the mark on the wall disappeared.

Once the boy made sure everything looked as it should, he snapped the notebook shut.

"All done…," he murmured to himself as he placed the notebook back in his pocket and left the room behind, as though he had lost all interest in it.

And since that day, no one in that town ever saw a girl named Yurika ever again…

The Bizarre Cat

At first, this cryptid looks like any other stray cat, but the moment you pick it up, its body starts to elongate. It moves just like an inchworm but is wicked fast at getting away, so not much is known about it.

1. Miho Ishida (14 years old, middle school)

When did you see it?

"Um, I think maybe two weeks ago. It was when I was on the way home from cram school, so it must have been a little past nine o'clock at night. I'd just left my friend Nana, who goes to the same cram school as me, so I was walking down the alleyway alone."

Do you normally go that way?

"No, that alley doesn't have any streetlights, so my mom told me I'm not supposed to walk down it at night.

"But there was a TV show I really wanted to see that day, and I can get home five minutes faster using that route, so I took it."

So you saw it in the alley?

"Yes. But I didn't know what it was at first. I mean, the alley was so dark, I could barely see it.

"There's a flower bed there, and I thought someone had just forgotten a cardboard box in it."

So it's about as large as a cardboard box, then?

"Um, I didn't get a good look, but I think it was at least as big as one."

How did you know what it was?

"I didn't back then. After I went through there, I heard a voice suddenly come from behind me.

"It was cackling, like *keh-heh-heh*, and kind of high-pitched like it was taunting me.

"I heard the rumors, so I thought it might be *that* thing, but when I turned around, I didn't see anything.

"But the cardboard box in the flower bed was gone. So I think maybe it might have been that box I saw."

2. Hiroshi Katou (30 years old, office worker)

Do you go down that alleyway often?

"Yep, I do. I go on a daily jog after work, so that alley's part of my route."

When did you see it?

"I'd say about a month ago. It started raining out of nowhere while I was out on my run, so I took shelter under a tree in the alley.

"It was probably around nine o'clock, I think. It might've been later, who knows."

Where did you see it?

"The thing was up on a roof. You know how there are houses along the alley.

"While I was waiting for the rain to let up, I saw it on the roof of the building right in front of me.

"One of the rooms on the second floor was lit up, and it was on the roof right next to that window. I couldn't make it out clearly, though."

What did it look like?

"Uh, I didn't see it move or anything, but I guess it was as big as a cardboard box, and it was brown, too. Looked pretty fuzzy."

Did you see its eyes?

"Its eyes? Nah, I couldn't even tell where its face was. It was just curled up there on the roof, you know.

"But I did hear the thing kind of snicker at me, like with a *keh-heh-heh* sound.

"I'm pretty sure *that* thing is the only thing that'd laugh like that."

3. Satoru Murayama (19 years old, unemployed / not in school)

I heard from someone that the thing was on the roof of your house.

"Hmph. So what? What do you wanna know? I don't have anything I could tell you."

Is your room on the second floor? And facing the alleyway?

"So what if it is?"

It sits near there a lot. On top of the roof next to your room.

"Does it? I never noticed."

Did you really not?

"What are you implying?"

If you're hiding something, you might end up in a lot of trouble.

"Oh, you mean that rumor that's been going around?"

Maybe you won't run into any issues, or maybe

it'll end up being the exact opposite. So I'd really like you to tell me what you know.

"F-fine... I'll tell you the truth. But I'm not to blame—I at least know that."

Sure, then will you tell me what you know?

"I noticed it about three months ago. I was studying for college entrance exams in my room, as always.

"Then I heard this voice from outside.

"It was a sort of snicker that sounded like *keh-heh-heh*.

"Really got on my nerves, too, since it sounded as if the thing was taunting me.

"At first, I didn't know anything about that old wives' tale going around, so I just thought it was somebody laughing outside.

"I tried to ignore it, but it kept on laughing.

"Then I got fed up and headed over to open the window so I could tell off whoever it was.

"But when I looked out, I saw that thing just sitting there on the roof, not doing anything."

Was it creepy?

"Creepy? Uh, I thought it was bizarre but not creepy."

Then what happened after?

"Well, I didn't know what the thing was, but I could tell it wasn't normal, so I tried taking a picture.

"I went to grab my phone from my desk, but by the time I got back to the window, it was gone."

Did you see it only that day? Someone else said he saw it a month ago on the roof.

"Right, it probably likes that spot. It usually curls up and perches there.

"I always wanted to take a picture of it, but whenever I got my camera ready, it always ran off.

"I don't think anybody else has gotten a picture of it, either, right? That's what it said online when I did some research.

"I don't think it wants to leave any evidence it exists."

That might be the case.

So earlier you said you weren't to blame. What did you mean by that?

"Exactly what I said. It's not my fault the thing disappeared."

It disappeared?

"Yeah, about a week ago. I was annoyed, since studying wasn't going great.

"I think it was sometime past nine at night. Then that thing started snickering again.

"I was used to it, since I've heard it tons of times, but for some reason, it really got to me that day.

"So I opened the window and threw my book at it, and I shouted at it to shut up and go away.

"I've got lousy aim, so I didn't hit it, but I guess I scared it off, since it scrambled into the shadows."

And you haven't seen it since then?

"Before, I'd see it every other day, but not since then.

"It probably went somewhere else.

"Hey, you don't think I'm gonna be cursed or anything because I scared it, do you?

"The rumors on the internet said that if you make it upset, something bad will happen to you. Nothing's gonna happen to me, right?"

4. Youko Kobayashi (45 years old, elementary school teacher)

You think the stories are wrong?

"Yes, that's what I would say. I don't think the creature would think to dislike someone or have a grudge against anyone. I think it's harmless and just settled down in town. Don't you think so?"

How can you tell?

"Well, the rumors that something bad will happen if it dislikes you are all just rumors, aren't they?

"Not a single person has actually had anything bad happen to them.

"I'm not one to believe in urban legends, but if it does exist, I don't think it's evil."

You haven't seen it for yourself?

"No, I haven't. But the children talk about it quite a bit.

"Some of the kids said they saw it yesterday, though."

Yesterday? Could you introduce me to those kids?

"Sure I can, but what do you intend to do once you find the creature?"

Well...

"Do you have something to do with that thing? It doesn't seem like you're looking for it out of plain curiosity to me."

Well, I can't say I have nothing at all to do it with. But I've never seen it before—not even once.

"Then why in the world would you look for it?"

It has an ability no one else knows about.

"An ability? Now, what do you mean by that?"

It has the power to answer one question in its lifetime with exact accuracy...

There's something I really need to ask it.

"I see—so that's why. It sounds like you have something very important to ask, then.

"All right... Let's try to get you in touch with those kids."

5. Ai Mochizuki, Aya Mochizuki (12 years old and 8 years old, elementary students)

Ms. Kobayashi, your teacher, said you saw the thing yesterday.

"Uh-huh, I saw it."

"I did, too!"

Where did you see it?

"There's this little park near our house, and that's where we saw it. Aya, my little sister, always plays there, but she didn't come home yesterday even when it got dark, so Mom told me to go get her for dinner."

So you saw it at the park at that time?

"I think it was around six. I was heading over to Aya while she was on the swings when I heard a weird voice from the grass behind me.

"It was going, like, *keh-heh-heh*, so I just had to find out what it was before I went home.

"When I heard it, too, I thought maybe it was *that*

thing. Everyone's talking about it at school, and lots of people online said that's what it sounded like. So then Aya and me looked around in the grass for it."

Did you find it?

"Yeah, it was on top of a cinder-block wall after we walked through the grass a little."

"It was curled up there and kinda crouching down."

"I was surprised it was actually there, but Aya seemed happy to find it and tried going closer."

"That's 'cause I wanted to pet it. It had this really fuzzy brown fur, and it was as big as a cardboard box. It looked super soft, too."

Did you do it? Touch it, that is?

"No, I tried to, but when I got close, its ears whipped up, and it suddenly leaped to the ground."

It leaped?

"Both of us were really shocked by that. Lots of kids at school have seen this thing, too, but they all said it was just curled up and sitting down. Also, most of them saw it at night, and no one else has seen it actually move."

How did it move?

"Well, you know how we said it's as big as a cardboard box? I was watching it and kind of worried about whether it'd land okay, but it suddenly went from being round to being really long. It stretched out just like an accordion. The wall was about a whole yard high, and it left its back legs on top while its front legs stretched down to the ground."

"Uh-huh, it went from being a cardboard box to really long and thin like a baguette."

"Then after its back legs reached the ground, it started to move like an inchworm across the ground by stretching and shrinking its body. Then it disappeared into the grass. It was really fast, too. You have no idea how amazed I was."

So do you think that scared it away?

"I think it's still around."

Why's that?

"Well, one of the girls in my class said so. This morning she heard the *keh-heh-heh* laugh."

I see. Thank you.

Also, did either of you see its eyes?

"Its eyes? Actually, I don't think we saw its face."

"Nuh-uh, I only saw its ears."

"But it did look exactly like everyone else said. Like a bizarre cat. It really did look like a huge, weirdly shaped cat."

It was twilight.

A lone boy made his way to a small park near an elementary school. He wore a red hood.

No one else was in the park.

In the grass behind the swing set…

The boy went over to the spot the girls had described to him. He found the grass behind the swings and walked a ways until he came across the wall.

Just the day before, the bizarre cat had been here, but the boy saw no sign of the cat now. *Maybe it really has wandered somewhere else*, the boy thought as he looked around.

Keh-heh-heh.

Suddenly, he heard a high-pitched, taunting laugh from the park.

"It's here! But where?!"

The boy left the grass and headed back into the park to resume his search. Then, as he was looking around, he found something about as big as a cardboard box on top of the slide.

It was fuzzy with brown fur.

"The bizarre cat!"

The boy ran over to it.

Twitch!

It seemed like the cat had noticed the boy, since its ears

pricked up as it sat curled up on the slide. It kept making that sound, "*Keh-heh-heh,*" but started to run away.

"Wait! Stop right there!" the boy yelled at the cat.

The bizarre cat seemed surprised when he addressed it. It flinched but stopped.

Mrooooowr.

This time it snarled like an actual cat as it raised its head and turned to face the boy.

Its eyes started to glitter.

The boy looked straight into its eyes as he said, "You have the power to answer just one question in your life with perfect accuracy. And the only person who can ask you that question is someone who's seen your eyes."

The boy approached the bizarre cat. As though it had accepted the boy, the creature remained perfectly still on the slide. It only stared at him with its glimmering eyes and didn't attempt to run.

Once the boy stood in front of the slide, he took in a deep breath and looked straight at the cat.

"O bizarre cat, where is the faceless kid?"

The boy shouted his question at the creature.

Then the cat opened its mouth wide.

Mrooooowr!!!

As the cat let out a low, rumbly snarl, it started to quiver all over.

Mroowr! "The...the..."
Mroowr! "The...the..."

In between its snarls, it began to speak in a human language.

The boy continued to stare right at the bizarre cat.

"The faceless kid... is...is..."

But in the next moment, the cat's eyes went wide.

Mroooowr!!!

As the cat screeched, its body began to stretch up into the air.

It grew longer and longer and thinner and thinner as it went up and up.

Soon it was even thinner than a baguette, then even thinner than a rope.

Mrooowr! Mroooooowr!

Once it was thinner than a rope, it cried out its loudest yet, and then, like a soap bubble, its whole body popped.

"Agh!" the boy yelled when he saw this.

The bizarre cat had disappeared.

"I should have known asking about the faceless kid wouldn't work…" Even though the boy was disappointed, he whipped out his bright-red notebook from his pocket. "So some things you make aren't dangerous…"

The boy opened the notebook and held the pages up to the slide where the cat had once been. A strange mark was carved into one of the slide's iron poles.

As the boy looked at it, he chanted a spell:

"ɘνloƨɘꓤ"

The mark glittered, inverted, and copied itself onto the open pages of the notebook. Then the mark on the pole disappeared.

The boy confirmed it was gone and shut his red notebook before putting it back into his pocket.

"I don't have anything else to do in this town…," he said, and left the park.

After that, the bizarre cat was never seen in that town again.

Love Spells

If you write an e-mail to <u>KAMISAMA@LOVE.MAIL</u> with
your crush's name in the subject line and your wish in the
body, then send it, you'll get an error message back. Delete
the error in your inbox and save only the e-mail you sent.
If you do this, your wish will come true.

Cancel

Yuuma Yama

To: <u>KAMISAMA@love.mail</u>

Cc/Bcc, sender: "panda.6

Subject: Yuuma Yamashit

I wish he liked me bac

"Ugh, why do I have to be such a coward?"

Alone in the girls' bathroom at her middle school, Misato Taniguchi sighed into the mirror she was looking at. Misato's reflection looked as dejected as she was.

It was all because of how things had gone during her school club meeting earlier.

Misato was in her first year of middle school, and she was a member of the tennis club. She wasn't athletic at all, but because she was in the club with her friend Nanami Shibata, every single day was fun. She also got along with the other kids in her grade, and the older students were all nice, too.

But what Misato looked forward to the most each week was when they had joint practice with the boys. Normally, the clubs practiced separately, but just once a week, they would have one session together.

Misato was really excited to be near the older boy she liked in the tennis club.

Yuuma Yamashita. He was the boys' tennis club captain. He had smooth brown hair and healthy, tan skin. His eyes were sharp, the bridge of his nose was high, and whenever his mouth opened, she saw the flash of his white teeth.

During those weekly sessions, Yamashita would teach Misato and the rest of the first-year students. He was serious and strict, but sometimes he would crack a joke, and he was always kind and cool.

Misato fell for him right away.

Whenever they had joint practices, Misato would try to get to know him better. But she was terrible at talking to people and hadn't spoken with boys very much, so months had gone by, and she still hadn't managed a single decent conversation with him.

Misato liked anime, but Yamashita probably wouldn't be interested in that.

But she had promised herself today that she would definitely approach him at the joint practice.

But I still didn't…

That day, Misato had been even more nervous than usual. Yamashita had shown up, but she didn't manage to say a word to him even after practice had come and gone.

At this rate, no matter how much time passes, he'll never get to know me…

Misato sighed loudly and dejectedly left the bathroom.

Once tennis club was over, she typically headed home with Nanami.

When she left the bathroom, she went to the school gate where her friend was waiting.

"Sorry for the wait!"

To keep Nanami from noticing, Misato pretended to be extra cheerful.

She hadn't told her that she liked Yamashita, and she didn't want to deal with Nanami asking why she was feeling down.

Then she noticed that Nanami was staring hard at her phone while she stood in front of the school gate.

"Are you playing a game?" Misato asked. Nanami shook her head and smiled.

"I was just doing something for good luck. Misato, do you know about the *kamisama* e-mail?"

"The kamisama e-mail?"

Misato had never heard of anything like that.

"One of my friends from class showed it to me," Nanami said. "It's a love spell thing you can do on your phone. When you do it, supposedly your crush will immediately start to like you."

"Uh, immediately? How do you do it?" Right away, Misato was very interested in that spell.

"It's pretty easy." Nanami showed her phone to Misato. "First you open up a new e-mail and write kamisama@ love.mail for the recipient. Then the subject is supposed to be the name of the person you like, and you write things like 'I want to go on a date' or 'I want us to go out' in the message, and then you send it."

"You send it? Will it actually reach anyone if you use that address?"

She doubted that "love.mail" was a real domain name.

But Nanami casually replied, "It doesn't go anywhere."

"It comes right back with an error," Nanami told her, "but that's the important part. Then you delete the error message and keep only the one you sent. If you do that, the thing you wrote in the message will come true."

Nanami showed her the e-mail.

The subject said, "Masato Ayano," and the body said, "I wish we would go on a date."

"Masato Ayano?" Misato asked.

"A boy I go to cram school with. We've been talking a lot, and I started thinking it might be nice if we went out."

Apparently, Nanami had been writing this message on her phone earlier.

"Do you think it really will come true?" Misato asked.

"Yeah. The classmate who told me about it said that it worked for her, and she went on a date with her crush."

"Really...?"

Misato was surprised by the whole thing and almost couldn't believe it. If the spell actually worked, then maybe she could go out with Yamashita sooner than she'd thought.

But I doubt it could be that easy...

As Misato wondered that, a smile formed on her face.

"You like someone, too, don't you, Misato?" Nanami asked.

"Huh?"

"It's written all over your face. C'mon, who is it?"

"Well, it's…" She started to say Yamashita's name, but she was so embarrassed that she couldn't manage it.

Nanami had a crush on a boy she talked to a lot, but Misato had barely ever said a word to Yamashita.

"I don't have a crush or anything…," Misato answered instead.

Evening on the same day.

Misato was doing her homework in her room, but she couldn't get the kamisama e-mail out of her mind.

If it really does grant wishes, then I should try it…

Misato stared at her phone, which was at the corner of her desk, but she still wasn't sure it would work.

Right then, she got a message on her phone.

"It's from Nanami…"

Misato read the message.

Nanami: It worked!

That was all it said.

Misato immediately messaged her back, **What happened?!**

Then the reply came in.

Nanami: I'm going on a date with Masato! It's all thanks to the kamisama e-mail!

"No way…"
Misato's eyes went wide.
So the love spell actually works?
Suddenly, Misato brightened.
"Then I'll try it, too!"
Now that her faith in it was ignited, she immediately opened a new e-mail message and entered "kamisama@love.mail" in the recipient and "Yuuma Yamashita" in the subject line.
Okay, so now it's just the message text…
She had no idea what to write once she got to that point.
Nanami had asked to go on a date with a boy she was already friends with. On the other hand, Misato had barely even had a conversation with Yamashita.
I can't just go out with him straight away…
Even if they went somewhere together, she doubted they would find anything to talk about. So even if she managed to get a date with him, he might end up liking her less.
Misato thought over what to write.

The important thing is for us to get to know each other first. So the first thing we should do is…

Right at that moment, Misato had the perfect idea.

I know! Talking! We just need to get to the point where we can talk with each other!

If she managed to talk with him, then they'd naturally progress to a point where they could go out.

So she wrote in the body of the e-mail, "I want to be able to talk to Yamashita and get to know him better!" Then she sent the e-mail.

The error message came back right away.

"I'm supposed to delete this, right?"

Misato carefully tapped the delete button.

"And if I keep the e-mail I sent, my wish should come true…"

In her mind, Misato repeated her wish to herself as she saved the message.

The next day.

Misato's heart pounded as she headed to school. Yamashita went to school the same way she did, so they'd run into each other at a particular intersection pretty often.

At that intersection, there was an optometrist with a sign that had a large drawing of glasses on it, so everyone called it the glasses-sign crossing.

Even though Misato saw Yamashita there sometimes, she never said hello to him and only ever watched him from afar.

But today will be different!

Misato believed her wish would be granted and Yamashita would talk to her.

Eventually, she got to the glasses sign and stopped to wait for the light to change. About a dozen other people were at the intersection as well.

Misato looked around for Yamashita.

"There he is!"

Yamashita was at the edge of the crowd waiting for the crosswalk signal. Misato moved closer to him so he would notice her.

But right then another boy came over to Yamashita.

"Morning," the boy said.

"Hey, morning."

He was another member of the tennis club. Yamashita was so preoccupied with talking to the other boy that he hadn't even noticed Misato, who was right behind him.

The light turned from red to green, and Yamashita started to cross with the other boy.

Oh no…

Maybe the love spell didn't actually work?

Misato deflated again and looked down at the ground.

"Taniguchi, right?" someone unexpectedly said to her.

Misato raised her face and saw that Yamashita had

Compose New E-mail

KAMISAMA@LOVE.MAIL

want to be able to talk to Yamashita and get to know him better!

stopped and was looking right at her.

"Uh, um." She faltered.

"Do you not recognize me? C'mon, I'm in the boys' tennis club."

"I—I know! You're Yamashita!"

"So you do know who I am. You go to school this way, too?"

"Y-yes. Oh, good morning!" Misato quickly bobbed her head in greeting.

"Yeah, morning. Right, how about we walk together, since we're both already headed in that direction?"

"What?"

"You don't want to?"

"N-no, I do. I'd like that!"

Misato felt out of sorts from how suddenly everything was happening, but at the same time, a smile formed on her face before she even realized it.

The spell worked…

Once Misato realized the kamisama e-mail actually worked, she quickly ran over to Yamashita.

From that day on, she began talking with Yamashita and got to know him.

When they had had joint practices together, Yamashita had noticed Misato talking with Nanami about anime, and he'd become interested in talking to her. Apparently, he liked anime, too, but he didn't have friends who were into it and hadn't had anyone else to chat with until then.

"The *Princess of Tennis* is really good."

"Uh-huh, all the characters are super cute. I've been watching it since the first season!"

Misato and Yamashita shared their thoughts about anime every day on their way to school.

"I'm glad we're friends, Taniguchi," Yamashita said.

"Do you mean it? I am, too. I'm happy that we started talking!"

Misato didn't care about the anime they talked about. She only cared that they were getting to know each other.

That was what really made her happy.

But after a month had gone by, she started to feel unsatisfied with their relationship.

She had a conversation with Yamashita every morning, but they never went beyond that.

But the only point of talking was so we could go on a date…

It was almost as though Yamashita didn't see Misato in that way at all. To him, she was just an underclassman who was a fellow anime fan.

This isn't enough!

Misato really wanted their relationship to move forward.

"So there's something I wanted to ask you," she said to Nanami after they'd finished with tennis club.

"What is it?"

"It's about the kamisama e-mail thing. Is it okay to send a second one about the same person?"

Misato was thinking of sending a new e-mail to wish for a date with Yamashita. She didn't know the rules, so she'd decided to run it by Nanami first.

"What? Did you send an e-mail, too?"

"Um, no, I just wanted to double-check."

Misato hadn't told Nanami about Yamashita yet. She'd only talked to Yamashita about anime so far, and she thought Nanami would laugh at her if she found out.

"What do you think? Is it okay to send a second one?" Misato asked, but Nanami just shook her head.

"Sorry, but apparently it's only one wish per person. One of my classmates tried to send a second one…"

"Okay, and what happened?"

"Then the first wish stopped working, too, and the boy she'd gotten to know hated her guts after that."

"What…?"

If I can't make a second wish, then I'll only be conversation buddies with Yamashita forever…

Misato had no idea what to do.

After she and Nanami parted ways on the walk home, she wallowed all alone.

I want a date with Yamashita… But I couldn't ever ask him out myself.

Now she regretted not having the courage to write "I want to go on a date" from the start.

Eventually, she reached a street near her home. There, she noticed a boy and girl in high school uniforms standing a short distance away.

The girl was Kayo Hashimoto, who lived in the neighborhood. Misato, who was an only child, had looked up to Kayo as if she were an older sister since she was little.

I wonder what Kayo is doing.

The boy next to Kayo was tall, and they were chatting together.

After a while, they went separate ways, and Kayo smiled and struck up a conversation with Misato.

"Misato, are you on your way home?"

"Yeah, but who was that just now, Kayo?"

"Oh, he's my boyfriend. I was always the only one with feelings, but we've been dating since last month."

"Wow, really?!" Misato said in surprise.

Kayo was about as shy as Misato and rarely talked to boys. Misato had never heard of Kayo having a boyfriend before.

"I'm so happy for you!" Misato said, and Kayo smiled and said, "Thank you."

"I think it's because of that love spell message," Kayo said.

"A love spell?"

"There's this 5151 love spell thing. I tried it out, and then we started dating."

This was her first time hearing about a love spell other than the kamisama e-mail.

"It's really popular at my school right now. I know—I can show you how to do it."

"Huh?"

Misato thought for just a moment but then answered, "Yeah, show me!"

The 5151 spell was a lot like the kamisama e-mail.

The only differences were that you would send the message to yourself and write the name of the person you liked in the subject, then 5151 in the message itself. After you sent the message, you would delete the bounce-back and save the initial message you sent.

Once Misato got all the instructions, she headed home and pulled her phone from her bag.

If she sent two e-mails using the kamisama e-mail method, she'd end up with neither wish and her crush would start hating her, but if she used another love spell, maybe her wish wouldn't be revoked.

Now I'll be able to get a date with Yamashita!

She couldn't write her own custom wish using the 5151 spell, but she thought she would definitely get closer to Yamashita this way.

She tried it immediately.

The next day.

Misato was at the glasses sign.

She normally met Yamashita there and they'd begin their anime catch-up. While she was looking around for him, she glanced over at the lights.

"Morning," she heard someone say from behind her.

It was Yamashita.

"Good morning!" Misato greeted him back and headed over to his side.

I wonder if he'll ask me out…

Misato's heart pounded in her chest as she waited for Yamashita to say something.

"Say, Taniguchi," he said.

"Yes?!"

"Did you watch *Princess of Tennis* yesterday?"

"Huh?"

"You haven't, then?"

"N-no, I did…"

"That match was amazing, wasn't it? I had no idea that was how it'd turn out!" Yamashita said, and he continued talking about anime just like usual.

The light turned green, and Yamashita started crossing. As Misato watched him walk away, her face fell without her even realizing it.

But why…? I know I followed all the instructions…

Maybe the 5151 spell didn't actually work?

While Misato wallowed in disappointment, she started to cross the street.

"Oh, right, Taniguchi," Yamashita suddenly said, as though he'd just remembered something. He looked over at Misato. "Are you free this Sunday?"

"Sunday? I have club in the morning, but I don't have anything in the afternoon…"

"In that case, want to head to an anime shop with me after club is over? I want to buy *Princess of Tennis* merch, then we can eat cake after. It'll be my treat, of course."

Huh? An anime shop? And even cake?!

When Yamashita suggested that out of nowhere, Misato looked all around.

"Uh, um, you mean just the two of us?" she asked.

"Yeah, of course. If you don't want us to be alone, then you can invite another friend, too."

"Oh, no! I'm fine with just us two!" Misato said in a hurry.

This…this is a date, isn't it? Then Yamashita just asked me out on a date?! I did it! I've really done it!

The love spell really *had* worked.

Misato kept yelling in her head to herself over and over again, *It's happening!* She was getting excited.

"What?! You liked Yamashita this whole time, Misato?!"

It was break time.

Misato had gone to the classroom next door to see Nanami and to tell her about what had happened that morning. Nanami was surprised that Misato's crush was someone she knew.

"I used both the kamisama e-mail and the 5151 spell to finally get a date with him!"

Misato explained how she'd used the two love spells.

"Right, I hadn't even thought of trying that."

"Isn't it brilliant?!"

"Yeah, it is. Now spring has finally come for you, too!"

"Spring?"

"They say spring comes for people who are in love. You're going to be so happy, Misato!"

"Yeah, thank you!"

Misato really was filled with happiness now that her wish had finally come true.

That evening.

Misato had finished tennis club and was on her way home when she decided to make a detour to Kayo's house. She wanted to let Kayo know that the love spell had worked for her.

Half of the credit should go to Kayo, after all! Misato thought as she walked up to Kayo's house, but when she got there, she saw Kayo talking to a boy at the front gate.

It wasn't the tall high school boy from last time. Instead, it was a young boy of average height wearing red clothes and a red hood over his head.

"Oh, Misato! Perfect timing." Kayo waved Misato down as soon as she noticed her.

The boy next to her turned to look at Misato, too. Under his hood, she could see that his skin was pale and he had large and clear eyes, a straight nose, and handsome but thin lips.

He seemed closer to Misato's age and maybe in middle school.

Who is he? I don't think he goes to my school.

As Misato was thinking, Kayo said, "He's looking into the love spell."

"Looking into it?" Misato cocked her head quizzically.

The boy asked her, "Do you know anything about it? She told me about the 5151 love spell, but apparently, there's one more going around town, too."

"Do you mean the kamisama e-mail?" Misato said without thinking anything of it. This earned her an intense stare from the boy.

"You know about it, then?"

His eyes looked serious.

Even though Misato was shaken by his expression, she still answered, "I don't just know about it. I actually used it. Oh, and I used the 5151 spell that you taught me on the same person, Kayo!"

"You did what?!" the boy suddenly shouted. "You used both methods on one person?!"

"Y-yeah… I did…"

"Do you know what you've done?"

The boy narrowed his large eyes and glared at her.

"What do you mean by that?!"

"When you use two spells in combination, you're in for trouble."

"What?!"

"You've mixed two spells that were never supposed to have been used together."

* * *

Misato felt a shiver go down her spine. Kayo quickly intervened when she saw the state Misato was in.

"What happens when you use them both?!"

The boy simply looked at Kayo, his eyes still narrowed.

"Anyone who mixes the two spells…" At that point, the boy paused.

"What happens?" Kayo nervously asked.

"Anyone who mixes the two spells will face misfortune," the boy said, looking straight at Kayo.

"Misfortune?"

"Kayo, I…" Misato was suddenly scared and gripped Kayo's sleeve.

"It'll be okay. There's no way that's true."

When Kayo realized Misato was afraid, she gave her a gentle smile.

"Do you think it's funny to scare a girl?" Kayo tried to scold the boy, but he'd already disappeared. "Huh? Where'd he go?"

"What? He's gone."

Right when they'd taken their eyes off him, he'd disappeared.

Misato and Kayo searched for him, but in the end, they were never able to find him.

The next day.

As Misato was on her way to school, she remembered what the boy had said the day before.

"Anyone who mixes the two spells will face misfortune."

I wonder what will happen to me. I'm kind of freaked out...

Right after their encounter, Kayo had told her the boy was just trying to mess with them, but Misato was unconvinced. His eyes had looked serious, and she doubted he was lying.

But how did he know so much about the spells...?

She had no idea who he was, but it seemed as though he knew a lot more about the spells than either she or Kayo did. As Misato mulled that over, she reached the intersection with the glasses sign. Yamashita was also at the edge of the intersection and waiting for the light to turn. When he noticed her, he smiled.

"Yamashita!"

Misato's worries were all behind her as she ran over to Yamashita.

Buzz, buzz.

Then, suddenly, her phone started to vibrate.

"Who would call me this early?" Misato stopped and pulled her phone out of her bag.

She saw she'd gotten a message, but the sender field was blank.

"What is this?"

Misato opened the message, curious about what she would find.

Then…

"θ#&✕$♂?;∫∫☆#✕#&✕$◇ ¥#&✕"

The message was in characters she couldn't understand at all.

"Wh-what is this supposed to be?"

It felt creepy.

"What's wrong?" Yamashita asked her.

"L-look at this." Misato tried to show him the message, even though she was frightened.

Right then, she got a new message. This time it was a drawing of a bloody skull.

Then she received several more in a row.

"Aaaah!" She was so scared, she unconsciously let out a scream.

"Taniguchi!"

When Yamashita realized Misato was terrified by whatever she'd seen on her phone, he quickly looked at the screen himself, but then he tilted his head dubiously.

"Taniguchi, what are you so scared of?"

"Huh?" Misato took another look at her phone, only to find it was blank. "How could that be…?"

She tried searching through her phone, but she couldn't find any sign of the message from earlier or the drawings.

"What happened…?"

She couldn't understand any of it. All she could do was stand frozen to the spot, dumbfounded.

After school.

Misato skipped practice and immediately headed to Kayo's

house. She'd decided to consult Kayo about the message from that morning.

Something was off.

She doubted she could ask Yamashita or Nanami for help, since they didn't know the whole story.

The only person I can count on is Kayo!

Once Misato was at Kayo's house, she pressed the button on their security doorbell.

"Yes, who is it?" came Kayo's mom's voice from the interphone.

"Um, it's Misato. Is Kayo in?"

Since Kayo wasn't part of a club, she should have been home by then, but her mom said, "Sorry, Misato, she's been feeling unwell since morning and hasn't gotten out of bed."

"What?"

"We had a doctor pay a home visit, but she couldn't figure out what was wrong, either. She's sleeping right now, so once she's feeling better, I'll have her get back to you," Kayo's mom said, then the line abruptly went dead.

She's not feeling well? And they don't know why...?

What had happened? Kayo had been just fine the day before.

Is it because I mixed the two love spells?!

Misato suddenly felt her stomach drop.

* * *

Buzz, buzz.

Then her phone started going off again. This time, the screen displayed the notification "Restricted Number."

Someone was calling her.

"But who?"

Misato didn't know anyone who would call her on a restricted number like this. She couldn't not pick up, so she took the call to see who it was.

"Hello…?"

"Ah…aah…ah…ah…"

On the other side of the phone, she heard a creepy groan. It wasn't Nanami or Kayo. It sounded like a girl's voice, but she didn't recognize it.

"H-hello?!"

Even though Misato was frightened, she tried to talk to the girl again.

"Ah…aaah…ah… Un…for…giv…able…"

"Huh?!"

Then the call ended.

"Wh-what was that?!"

She pulled her phone away from her ear immediately, not understanding what had just happened.

Then the phone started buzzing again. She'd gotten an e-mail this time.

On top of that, even though Misato hadn't done anything at all, it opened all on its own and displayed on the screen.

"What's going on?!"

Misato automatically looked at the screen.

The message had no subject or body and only contained an image. This time it was of a creepy girl with long hair. Her eyes looked like they were filled with hate as they stared straight into the camera—and she wasn't the only one. Behind her, several other similar creepy girls were ruefully staring at her through the screen.

"Aaaah!"

Misato was so frightened, she couldn't bear to look at the photo any longer.

But right at that moment, she saw something behind the girls—it was a sign with an illustration of a giant pair of glasses. The girls were standing in front of that sign.

"Wait, isn't that—?"

All the blood felt as if it'd drained from her body.

The photo had been taken at the intersection she normally went to.

"No!"

Misato ran straight back home.

Kayo's house was only two left turns away from Misato's.

If she walked, she could get there in three minutes, or one if she ran.

And so Misato ran as fast as she could as she went around the first corner and headed straight for the next one.

But someone was already there.

"Oh!"

Misato's eyes went wide as saucers when she saw the person.

It was the same creepy girl she'd seen in the picture.

As though the girl had been waiting for her, she turned to Misato and stared through the gaps of the long hair that hid her face.

"Aaaah!"

Misato knew she would be in trouble if the girl caught her.

As her instincts raised an alarm, she quickly tried to head back the way she'd come. But another creepy girl stood on the corner behind her, too. Just like the first girl, she glowered at Misato through the strands of her hair. The two girls' eyes never left Misato as they steadily drew closer to her.

"No...no...," Misato said.

In that moment, Misato felt her phone vibrate in her hand,

and even though she hadn't answered, her phone picked up the call, and a voice came through:

"Ah...aah...ah...ah..."

It was the same creepy girl's voice.

"Wait, is this voice…?"

Misato looked ahead of her and realized the girl approaching her was mouthing something.

Her lips matched the voice on the phone exactly.

"Unforgivable...unforgivable...unforgivable..."

The girl right in front of her was speaking to her through the phone.

"Aaaaaaah!"

Misato threw her phone and dashed toward the main road, away from the girls.

It was now five o'clock in the evening.

Misato ran as she searched for help, but she could find no one on the road.

"What's going on?!"

Normally, the street was filled with students and housewives on the way home from grocery shopping.

Right now, though, the streets were empty.

"Help! Help me!"

Misato kept running, desperate to find someone, anyone.

Then she saw a figure standing up ahead.

"I found someone!"

She sprinted at full speed toward them.

"Please help me!" Misato yelled.

But the next moment, Misato was in for another shock.

The person standing in front of her had been another creepy girl all along.

"Noooo!!!"

Misato scrambled away.

Just then, someone suddenly grabbed her arm from around a street corner.

"Aah!"

She automatically started to struggle, thinking it was one of those creepy girls.

"Calm down!"

But instead she heard a boy's voice. On top of that, she recognized it.

Misato turned toward him and saw the boy she had met the day before.

"Help me!" she cried.

She had no idea who he was, but he was the only one she could ask for help. Misato clung to the boy.

"I thought it'd end up like this…," the boy said without batting an eye.

"What do you mean by that?"

"If this keeps up, you'll end up killed by the apparitions."

"A-apparitions?!"

Misato had no idea what the boy was talking about.

"Anyway, we're in danger if we stay here. C'mon, this way."

"Hey! Wait!"

The boy pulled Misato down an alley.

Once they were in a side street, Misato took another look at the boy.

"Who were those girls? You called them apparitions…"

"Yeah. Those are the apparitions of the girls who had their hearts broken because someone else's love spell worked."

"They had their hearts broken…"

When someone used a love spell, they would gain love, but on the other hand, they would also break someone else's heart.

"Because you combined two spells, the apparitions manifested in this world. They hate people who have successful relationships, like you. If you're caught, you're not escaping with your life."

"What…?" Misato finally realized how serious her mistake was. "Then what do I do?"

The boy seemed to know a lot about love spells for some reason. So she assumed he'd know how to help her, too, and she started to feel as though her fate depended on him.

The boy let out a small sigh and murmured, "Fine." Then he added, "I wanted to get this sorted out before the apparitions appeared, though…"

"What?" Misato still had no idea what the boy was talking about, but he launched into an explanation of how to get rid of the apparitions.

"You need to use the phone you sent those e-mails on to send another e-mail to yourself. Send the number 030, then all the apparitions with disappear. It's kind of like an SOS to get rid of ghosts."

Then the boy said, "Well, hurry up."

"Uh, sure, okay!" Misato said, quickly reaching for her phone, only to realize she didn't have it. "Oh!"

"What's wrong?"

"I…tossed my phone on the street."

Misato had been so scared of the phone call from the girl that she'd flung her phone away.

"Ugh! How much more trouble are you going to stir up?" the boy said.

"That's not helping things…"

"We're going to go get it right now. Show me where it is!"

Misato nodded and headed out of the alleyway with the boy.

Once they got to the main road, Misato started to run

toward where she'd thrown her phone, but along the way, she saw a giant crowd of people up ahead.

They were the creepy girls. There were at least ten of them—no, maybe even twenty. All of them staggered toward Misato like zombies.

"There are so many of them…"

"And there'll be more coming to try to catch you. If we don't hurry, you won't be able to get away from them anymore."

Even though she was scared, Misato kept running down the road. Then she felt uncertain. Why was it that no one else was around?

"Why aren't there other people around?" Misato asked the boy, who was running ahead of her.

"It's because of the apparitions. They're only after you, so they're making sure that anyone who could get in their way can't come near you."

"Is that why Kayo is in bed, too?"

"Yeah, it's to isolate you. So you can't ask anyone for help," the boy responded matter-of-factly.

"But…" Misato suddenly had a new question. "Then how are you still here?!"

If the apparitions were keeping everyone else away from Misato, then how was it that the boy was right by her side?

The boy tilted his face just slightly and peered at Misato from the corners of his eyes.

"They can't force me away," he said.

"Why's that?"

"Well…" The boy started to explain but then trailed off. "That has nothing to do with you," he said, then he turned to face forward again and eventually stopped in his tracks. "This is it. So your cell phone is somewhere here?"

Misato realized they were at the alley near her house.

She looked around the area and found her phone.

"There it is!"

Misato was still curious about the boy, but she needed to get rid of the apparitions right away. That was more important.

"Hurry up and send a 030 e-mail!"

"Okay!" Misato raced over and reached for her phone.

Snatch!

Right as Misato grabbed her phone, someone had also grabbed her arm.

She looked up to see a creepy girl hiding behind a utility pole.

The girl crawled over and stared her down as she kept a tight hold of Misato's arm.

"Get off!"

"Darn it! No!"

The boy rushed over to Misato and pried the girl's hand off.

"Aaaaaaah!!!"

She started to groan.

They looked around to see an uncountable number of creepy girls approaching them.

"Unforgivable...unforgivable... unforgivabllle!!!"

"Hurry up and send that e-mail!" the boy yelled.

"O-okay!"

Misato quickly opened her e-mail on her phone and entered her address and 030 into the message.

"Aaaaaaah!!!"

The girls were closing in around them. Right at the moment they were about to reach her, Misato tapped the send button.

"Ngh…nhh…"

When Misato opened her eyes, the sun had already set a long time ago and it was dark.

She'd fainted at some point.

"Where are the apparitions…?"

She looked around in a panic, but all the girls had disappeared. She turned and saw the boy standing by the utility pole. He was holding a red notebook in his hand and was doing something by the pole.

"You're awake?"

"Yeah…" Misato stared at the boy. "Who are you?"

He knew all about the love spells and was the only person who could come near Misato while the apparitions had kept her away from everyone else.

The boy looked directly at her and slowly said:

"I'm Fushigi Senno. I travel from town to town, hunting down urban legends."

"Urban legends?"

Misato thought he would explain, but Fushigi didn't say another word about it. Instead, he only told her about the love spell that had appeared in her town.

"Someone purposefully brought two love spells to this town in order to get someone here to mix them."

"What do you mean by that? You mean someone did all this on purpose?" Misato asked, but Fushigi didn't answer her question.

"Don't worry. Sending another love spell e-mail won't work anymore, not in this town. I've collected them all."

"What?"

"If you really want a love life, then you shouldn't rely on a spell. Sometimes love spells are haunted by girls with broken hearts," Fushigi said, then he left without another word.

Fushigi Senno...

She had no idea who he really was.

However, just like Fushigi said, after that, no matter how many times anyone sent love spell e-mails in that town, no wish was ever granted again...

SOMEONE'S NOTEBOOK

There is a cursed village no one

knows about. It's dangerous, so you must never

go near it, but even the most cautious person

has no way of knowing the name of the

village or where it's located.

That's because not a single person who

has entered the village has gotten out alive.

All the friends I came with are gone.

I'm the only one left now.

If you see this journal, run away immediatel

The village's name is

Sugisawa Village

A village that supposedly exists in the mountains of Aomori Prefecture. There is no clear way of getting to the village, but those who accidentally wander into it never return. Supposedly, the ghosts of the slaughtered villagers have haunted the place since they were all wiped out.

It was evening on a certain summer day. A single car drove along the mountain road that stretched endlessly, lined with green trees.

Mayu Hasegawa and her family had driven to the mountain.

"It's been a while since we've gone out on a drive with the whole family," Minako, Mayu's mom, who was in the passenger seat, said to her dad, Masafumi, who was driving.

"Yep. Work's been so busy, I just haven't been able to get a day off."

"But we only saw mountains," Mayu grumbled to her parents from the back seat.

They'd gone all the way to the summit, but she'd just seen mountains, mountains everywhere. So Mayu hadn't been very impressed with the scenery.

"Is that so? Well, I liked the view."

"That's right. We used to drive up to the peak so often when we were younger," Minako said.

To Masafumi and Minako, the mountains were filled with

memories. Mayu personally thought it was just another boring trip.

We should have gone to an amusement park if we were really going out.

Mayu glanced at her older brother, Kazuya, who was sitting next to her. He'd been playing a game on his phone since forever ago.

"Kazuya, you bored?"

"Guess so. I think I would've had more fun playing a game."

Kazuya, who was in his second year of middle school, didn't think going on a drive with his family was much fun. In fact, he'd been half-irritated about it from the start and acted as though he was only tagging along because he had to. On the other hand, Mayu, who was in the sixth grade, had been excited about it. She'd never gone to a mountain before except on short hikes, so she was looking forward to the trip, but it wasn't anything like what she had expected.

I can't believe it's been the same view no matter how far we go...

Even though her parents seemed to be thrilled, Mayu started to feel sick and tired of the trip.

Eventually, the sun started to set, and their surroundings dimmed.

For some reason, Minako started to become restless.

"How much longer until we get back into town?"

"Right, I think another hour?"

Minako looked worried when she heard that.

"But we're getting a delivery at five. Isn't there a shortcut we could take?" Minako said. Masafumi considered that as he glanced at the map displayed on the car navigation screen.

"A shortcut, huh…?" Suddenly, his face lit up. "Oh, looks like there's a turnoff up ahead. We might be able to get to the base of the mountain in half the time if we take that."

Mayu leaned forward from the back seat and took a look.

The screen showed another small road heading off the mountain path that led to the town without their needing to take the winding main road.

"All right, let's try going that way."

"Yes, let's."

And so, Mayu's family decided to take the shortcut.

"Hmm? What's that?"

Masafumi suddenly spoke as they approached the side road.

When everyone else looked in the same direction, they saw a boy standing alone at the entrance to the road.

"What's a little boy doing in a place like this?"

Mayu tilted her head quizzically. They'd gone pretty far down the mountain by car.

The only thing around them was more mountain. Few people were in the area, and they'd barely even come across other cars.

"Was he hiking up the mountain?" Mayu asked Masafumi.

"Probably not."

"Why's that?"

"Well, look at his clothes. That's not what I'd call hiking gear."

The boy was wearing red clothes with a red hood, as if he were just going for a walk around town. He didn't even have a backpack with him.

He really didn't seem to be on a hike, just like Masafumi had said.

"Maybe the car he was in broke down and he's looking for help?" Kazuya suggested as he peered into the distance.

"You think it's car trouble?!"

"Now that would be an emergency!"

Mayu and Minako both started to shout, and Masafumi nodded along.

"You might be onto something there. All right, let's go talk to him."

Masafumi pulled over by the boy.

"What are you doing here, bud?" Masafumi asked after rolling down his window. The boy looked at them.

He appeared to be about middle school age.

Under his hood, they could see that his skin was pale and that he had large and clear eyes, a straight nose, and handsome but thin lips.

This boy was Fushigi Senno.

"Did your car break down?" Masafumi asked him.

Mayu also opened her window and waited for him to reply, but Fushigi just shook his head slightly.

"Are you all going down this road?" the boy asked, glancing briefly to the road that continued behind him.

"Yeah, that's right," Masafumi replied, and Fushigi turned to look at him.

"You shouldn't go this way. There's a forbidden village you absolutely can't set foot in."

Mayu's entire family was confused when they heard that reply.

"A forbidden village? Now, what's that supposed to mean?" Masafumi asked the question that was on everyone's mind.

"Exactly what I said. If you head to the village, the people living there will attack you, and you'll never make it out again. There have already been people who have traveled this way and never made it home."

"You're kidding me…" Mayu couldn't believe anything Fushigi was saying. "Why would the villagers attack us?"

"They probably just don't like outsiders."

"What happens to the people who get attacked?"

"I think they're killed."

"No way!"

Mayu felt a shiver run through her.

"No way does a village like that exist!" Mayu yelled at him. She didn't like scary stories.

The expression on Fushigi's face didn't change one bit as he stared right at Mayu.

"I'm not invested in getting you to believe me, but I'm warning you not to go for your own sake. By the way, the name of the village is Sugi—"

"There's no such thing anyway!" Mayu cut Fushigi off because she was so upset. She looked over at Masafumi. "Dad, let's head back to the first road!"

"But we don't have time…"

"Who cares about that!"

Masafumi looked over at Fushigi when Mayu said that. "Want a lift?"

They saw Fushigi's lips move slightly from under the shade of his hood.

"Don't worry about me."

"If you say so…" Masafumi looked back at his family in the car and said, "Well, let's go back the way we came."

Then reversed the car to head back down the mountain road.

"What was with that kid…?" Mayu was the only one still irritated.

She looked again to see that Fushigi was headed the opposite way up the mountain road they were on, and when Masafumi noticed that, he asked, "Actually, want to try the side road anyway?"

Mayu stared at her father.

"Wait, what?"

"Don't you feel like checking it out now? Let's see if this forbidden village actually exists."

Masafumi was someone who liked spooky stories and mysteries.

"No way!" Mayu cried out.

"But you just said the village can't exist, Mayu. In that case, there shouldn't be anything wrong with taking the side road."

"I did, but…"

While Mayu was fretting, Kazuya chimed in, "I'm in." He was even smiling.

"Sounds like fun to me. Let's go!" Kazuya enjoyed a good mystery, too.

"What are you doing, Kazuya?!"

"Well, now that we're not supposed to go, I'm really itching to head over. If we actually find a village like that, we can just scram."

"Scram…? Seriously?"

Mayu looked over to Minako for help, but their mother was so exasperated by Masafumi that it seemed she'd given up on even commenting.

"Oh dear, boys will be boys, I suppose."

"Mom!"

"I'm not interested in finding out whether this village exists or not, but we need to get home soon, so let's take the side road."

Once Minako had given her permission, Masafumi nodded firmly.

"All right, let's head out!"

Masafumi stopped the car and made a U-turn.

Then he drove straight into the side road.

Even though Mayu hadn't wanted to go this way, she'd been overruled by everyone and couldn't say anything else.

They'd traveled down the road for about half an hour.

The sun was rapidly setting, and it was getting darker and darker.

The road was just large enough for a single car, so as they drove through, the trees and greenery seemed to surround them like walls on both sides.

"Are you sure there's a village on this road?"

If there really was one, then the villagers had to use this road on a daily basis, but it was overgrown with weeds, and they saw no traces of any cars traveling down the path regularly.

"Maybe that kid was lying?" Mayu said.

"He might have been" Masafumi replied. "Probably just trying to scare us…"

Right then, they saw something up ahead.

"Wait, is that…?" Kazuya leaned forward to get a better look.

They'd come across a tunnel just large enough for a single car.

"What's a tunnel doing in a place like this?"

It didn't seem to have any lights inside it, either.

"I wonder if the village is beyond it?"

"Hmm. All right, let's check it out!"

Kazuya and Masafumi were suddenly eager to enter, and the car lurched right forward.

"Wait!"

Even though Mayu was scared, they headed into the tunnel, which was cramped, long, and very dark.

"I can't see anything."

Masafumi turned on the car's headlights, but the illumination only reached the ground directly in front of the car, so they couldn't see what was up ahead.

"This thing sure seems long…"

"Yeah, it's a little creepy, too…"

Kazuya's and Masafumi's faces froze as they talked.

"Mom, I'm scared…"

"Everything's okay. We should be back in town at the base of the mountain soon," Minako said, but she seemed anxious.

Eventually, they could make out the exit ahead of them and were almost on the other side.

"Oh, thank goodness, that must be the exit!"

Mayu was so relieved, she let out a huge sigh.

They drove out of the tunnel and started going down a narrow side road just as they had earlier, only this road seemed to keep going on and on.

"Dad, are we not in town yet?"

"Uh, right, we've been driving for nearly thirty minutes, so we should have…"

Masafumi seemed confused, too, and cocked his head to the side.

"Huh?"

Suddenly, Minako let out a sound.

"What's wrong, Mom?" Mayu asked. Minako was looking at the car navigation screen.

"There's something not right with this."

"What's the problem?"

Mayu turned to look at the screen, too, and saw that it showed they were in the middle of the forest. They couldn't see any roads on it at all. The car seemed to be driving endlessly through the trees.

"Dad, why are we inside the woods right now?"

"Hmm? W-well, that's odd."

Right at that moment, the screen suddenly started to flicker.

"What's going on?"

Then it went dead.

"What just happened?"

Masafumi tried to turn it back on, but the screen remained completely black.

"Is it broken?"

"I've never seen this happen before…"

Masafumi tried all sorts of buttons, but the screen refused to turn on at all.

Even their TV screen and radio wouldn't respond.

"What's going on?!"

Mayu tilted her head.

Then Kazuya yelled right next to her, "Look at this!"

He showed his phone to everyone else. His device was also dead.

"The screen shut off out of nowhere, and I can't turn it back on."

Kazuya pressed all the buttons on his phone, but nothing happened.

"Are you sure you didn't let the battery die?"

"No way. It was fine when I checked earlier."

Mayu was wondering what could possibly be happening when Minako spoke up next. "Mine is dead, too!"

It looked as though Kazuya's phone wasn't the only one on the fritz. They checked Masafumi's, too, and even his was dead.

"What the heck is going on?"

They were all starting to feel creeped out.

"Something's off. We need to go back!"

"Uh, yeah, let's turn around!"

Masafumi drove quickly, looking for a spot where he could make a U-turn.

But right then…

Thunk!

Suddenly, a huge sound came from the car.

"Aah! What was that?!"

The whole car pitched forward. The road had suddenly started to slope down, and the car seemed to float in midair for a moment.

"Aaaah!" Mayu was so scared, she shrank back into her seat.

"Hey, look at that!" Kazuya yelled as he leaned forward.

Mayu looked ahead to see a village below the slope.

"Wait, is that really it?!"

It wasn't the town at the base of the mountain. They'd come across an unfamiliar little village.

Mayu grabbed the driver's seat from behind and audibly gulped. Maybe this was the village the boy they'd met earlier had talked about?

While Mayu wondered whether it could be possible, she felt the car start going down.

"I'm scared," she murmured, her face stiffened in fear. She glanced to the side of the road suddenly and saw a sign hidden behind the trees.

She could only make out *Sugi* on the sign since the rest

Welcome to Sugi Village!

was covered by leaves, but she knew for certain that was the first part of the village's name.

"Sugi… Wasn't that…?"

Mayu remembered what Fushigi had said.

"By the way, the name of the village is Sugi—"

"This really is it!"

Mayu was certain the place in front of them was the forbidden village.

Once they arrived in town, Mayu and Minako stayed in the car while Masafumi and Kazuya got out.

It was a small village of just ten or so wooden houses. The whole place was eerily silent, and not a single person was around. Some of the houses had run-down bicycles and rusted trucks in front of them, so the only thing they could glean was that people were living in the village. The spookiest detail of all was that even though it was still evening, every single house's shutters were closed.

"Something seems off."

"Yeah, this village is weird…"

Kazuya's and Masafumi's voices trembled.

The sky was growing darker and darker all the while as the sun was completely blotted out by the clouds.

"My, my, what do we have here?"

Suddenly, they heard a voice come from behind them.

Masafumi and Kazuya looked around with a start, as did Mayu and Minako in the car.

An old granny was standing behind them. Her entire face was wrinkled, and her eyes were nothing but thin lines peering out at them.

She appeared almost comical.

Mayu thought she looked a lot like a stereotypical old grandma from the countryside.

The woman stared at the family.

"Uh, um… We got a bit turned around," Masafumi explained as he took a step forward.

"Turned around? Ah, must've taken the side road, then. Oh-ho-ho…"

She let out a friendly laugh and approached the family.

Overcome by curiosity, Mayu and Minako abandoned both their anxiety and the car as they stepped out to join the others.

"Just go back the way you came," the woman said. "Should take you right back to that big mountain road you started on, but don't you go around speeding. Not unless you want to head off onto another path…"

"Another path?" Masafumi questioned her. "But there was only one side road."

However, the old woman didn't reply and gently smiled instead.

Mayu tried to recall the route they'd taken to the village. All she remembered were the trees growing thick around them and continuing on and on forever.

Had she missed a fork in the road?

As Mayu was thinking, Kazuya suddenly tapped her on the back, trying to draw her attention.

"Hey, look…" He motioned with his chin at a building a short distance away.

"What is it?" Mayu asked, and Kazuya pointed at the house's door.

"Isn't it open a little?"

"Yeah…"

"Look really closely inside."

"Inside?"

Mayu trained her eyes on the house. The sun was setting, so it was dark, but she could still make things out.

The door was slightly ajar.

Mayu noticed a giant pile of disheveled fabric inside.

"Those are clothes? Maybe they were taking in the laundry...?"

"No, look carefully!" Kazuya whispered, so Mayu tried again.

"Oh!" The next moment, Mayu was startled. The pile was illuminated by an indoor light, and every single scrap of fabric was stained bright red. "Wait, is that—?"

"Yeah, it's blood! It's blood!"

Mayu's eyes went wide before she caught herself.

"My, my, how unfortunate that you noticed."

At some point, the elderly woman had started watching Mayu and Kazuya.

"Well, now that you've seen them, I'm afraid—" The old woman's wrinkled face turned grim as she approached them.

"No! Get away from me!" Mayu bolted for the car.

"Dad! Mom! We need to go!" Kazuya yelled, and made a run for it, too.

"Mayu! Kazuya!"

Masafumi and Minako had noticed something was off and quickly followed their children.

Mayu, who got there first, tried to open the door, but at that moment, she sensed someone nearby. She looked and saw a large crowd of elderly people in the shadow of one of the houses.

"Aaaah!"

"Mayu!"

The rest of the family made it to the car, too.

Masafumi opened the door and immediately got into the driver's seat.

"Everyone, get in the car! Hurry!"

"Got it!"

After Masafumi made sure the entire family was safely inside, he tried to drive off.

Thump...thump... thump!

Before they could get away, the elderly mob started pounding on the car's doors.

"Stop!"

"Dang it!"

The group had started to bang on the windows and hood of the car, too.

"Dad, hurry!"

"I know! Outta the way!"

Masafumi honked the horn over and over as he plowed through the attackers surrounding the car and peeled out of there.

"Wh-what was that…?"

While they sped away, Mayu started to tear up from how scared she was.

If they'd stayed in the village, she was sure the old people would have captured them, too, and if they were caught, they would have been killed.

Mayu shivered, then she suddenly looked out at a building.

Her eyes settled on something she hadn't noticed when they'd first arrived.

"Wait, is that…?"

She saw lots of dolls nailed into one of the house's walls.

Some of them were headless, while others were charred black, and she even saw some that were bright red among the many, many dolls along the wall. Plus, she also saw the words *cursed* and *lock away* scrawled all over the walls and fences around the houses in something that looked a lot like red paint.

"What's wrong with this place…?"

When Mayu and her family realized how strange the village was, they all couldn't help but shudder.

They didn't slow as they fled, and once they reached the slope, they went back up it and onto the side road they'd come from.

They'd traveled down the side road for about ten minutes.

The area around them had become dark before they knew it.

Mayu and the others were finally feeling settled again, but they noticed something odd. No matter how far they drove, they never found the tunnel.

"It only took two or three minutes to get to the slope after we left the tunnel, right?"

"Yeah, I'm pretty sure."

They'd panicked when their navigation system and phones had stopped working, but the slope hadn't been very far from the tunnel.

"Why haven't we seen it yet, then…?"

Right at that moment, Mayu remembered what the old lady had said.

"Don't you go around speeding. Not unless you want to head off onto another road…"

"Wait a sec!" Mayu yelled, which seemed to jog Masafumi's memory, too. He appeared startled.

"So we're on a different road, then? How could that be…?"

They were racing down a long, narrow road that continued straight ahead.

"How would we take the wrong road?"

"I can't understand how we could, either…," Minako added after Kazuya.

However, no matter how far they went, they never reached the tunnel.

"Dad, what do we do?!"

Mayu was becoming more and more frightened. They'd gotten away from the forbidden village, but now they couldn't find their way back to the mountain road.

At that moment, Masafumi shouted, "Hey, look at that!"

They saw a village ahead of them. Unlike the last one, this village contained several newer buildings, and they saw people outside. It wasn't the town at the base of the mountain, but at least it wasn't creepy.

"Whew! We made it to a nearby village!"

"Yeah, this place looks like it's fine!"

They drove into the village and saw that all the buildings and people seemed perfectly ordinary.

Mayu's entire family felt relieved as they looked around.

"Okay, let's try asking someone how we can get back to the mountain road we came from," Masafumi said, and he parked the car in front of a store. He started up a conversation with the owner.

"Oh-ho, looks like you almost got yourselves in hot water." The friendly fiftysomething shop owner commiserated with them. "I'm scared to think we have a village like that so close to home… I'll need to warn the others around town. Could you point out the location to me later?"

"S-sure… But it's really close by, so I thought you'd already know about it," Mayu gingerly said, which made the shop owner laugh.

"Well, we never, ever leave town."

"Huh…?"

"Anyway, I'll go fetch a policeman, so why don't you tell him all about it," the shop owner said while beckoning Mayu's family in. She told them to wait and headed off.

"Haah… I can't believe what we've been through."

Once Mayu was inside the air-conditioned store, she relaxed slightly.

"Looks like that kid was telling the truth," Kazuya said, and Mayu nodded in agreement.

"That's why I said we should've gone down the first road."

"Sorry, really. Well, we're fine now, so it all worked out."

"It so *didn't* work out!"

Mayu and Minako glared at Masafumi—who didn't seem regretful in the slightest—as they took seats in the shop.

"But what did the shop owner mean earlier when she said they don't leave this village?"

"I guess they've got everything they need here and don't need to go anywhere else?"

"Huh, you think so? But it looks so empty here."

"Well, now that you mention it…," Minako said as she tilted her head quizzically.

Right then, Mayu noticed a notebook lying by a pay phone installed at the entrance of the shop.

"What's this doing here?"

The notebook seemed to be hidden between the phone and its base.

Mayu picked it up without thinking much of it.

It seemed pretty beat-up and old.

"What's it say?"

"Dunno."

Mayu headed back to her family, and they all looked at the notebook together.

X X X X X

There is a cursed village no one knows about. It's dangerous, so you must never go near it, but even the most cautious person has no way of knowing the name of the village or where it's located. That's because not a single person who has entered the village gets out alive. All the friends I came with are gone. I'm the only one left now. If you see this journal, run right now. The village's name is

X X X X X

"What is this?!"

The writing seemed to continue.

Mayu cocked her head as she turned the page.

And there, on that page, were the words:

Sugisawa Village!!!

The words were eerie, as though the person who had written them had been filled with fear.

As he looked at the writing, Kazuya blurted out, "Do you think this is about that village from earlier?"

They hadn't been able to read it properly because of the

trees blocking it, but the sign at the other village's entrance had said *Sugi* on it.

"Then someone who went through something scary while at that village must have written this?"

"Yeah, I think so."

"But what's it doing here?"

Mayu started to wonder why the notebook had been hidden at the pay phone.

"Well, I hadn't realized someone wrote something like that."

Suddenly, they heard a voice.

Mayu's entire family turned toward it and saw the shop owner standing nearby.

"Really now, they shouldn't have," she said as she glared at the family.

Behind her was an entire group of villagers. Half of them carried lit torches, and the other half held something very different—sickles, which were a grisly red from blood.

"Huh...?"

The sight of them filled Mayu with terror.

At the same time, she saw the sign behind the villagers. Lit by the torches, it said, WELCOME TO SUGISAWA!

"Wait, Sugisawa...?" Mayu murmured to herself, and the shop owner grinned.

"That's the name of our village, of course."

""""Welcome to Sugisawa.""""

The shop owner and the sickle-carrying mob gave this sinister greeting as they raised their weapons and closed in on Mayu and her family.

It was morning. A single car raced down a mountain road.

A middle-aged man sat in the driver's seat, along with his wife, who sat on the passenger side.

In the back was a boy wearing a red hood. It was Fushigi.

The couple had picked him up in their car while he'd been walking along the mountain road.

"Wow, a forbidden village, huh?"

The woman suddenly turned to Fushigi and asked, "But why are there two of them?"

"Well…" Fushigi began to explain. "One attacks anyone who wanders in, and the other one warns people not to enter that village. The village that attacks people is called Sugisawa Village, and the one that warns people is called Sugimoto Village. After Sugisawa Village attacks outsiders, they take them away somewhere."

"You can't be serious…"

"I am," Fushigi replied indifferently. "In the past, the entire village was murdered, and the villagers' ghosts all gather to attack anyone who happened to pass through. Ghosts can't escape the town, either, so anyone who enters it can never escape, either."

"What…?"

The woman had become frightened, so the man spoke in her place. "But the first village you come across on the side road is Sugimoto Village, right?"

"That's right," Fushigi said. "It's a small village where only the elderly live, and they have protective dolls and charms on all their walls and fences to quell the spirits in Sugisawa. They also apparently take the clothes of the people who have been attacked. They probably feel bad for them and hold a service for their clothes, if nothing else."

"So Sugimoto Village is filled with good people, then?"

"Yeah, as long as you listen to their warning, you'll make it home in one piece," Fushigi said, which made the man tilt his head.

"But you're on your way to Sugisawa right now? Are you sure you should be going there?"

Fushigi suddenly looked out the window.

"They only attack people at night. It's not dangerous if you're there in the daytime, but the road only appears at night, so you can't really get there during the day. I wasn't able to find it yesterday when I went."

"So then you might not find it today, either?"

"Maybe not."

"But why are you trying to go all the way to that village?"

"I need to collect something there."

"What's that?"

"Don't worry about it," Fushigi said as he grasped his red notebook. He planned to go to Sugisawa Village to collect the strange mark that would be carved somewhere there.

"Well, that's a pretty scary story, in any case," the woman said as she hugged herself.

After a while, they reached the side road, and Fushigi got out of the car.

"Are you sure we should drop you off here?"

"Yeah, thank you for taking me," Fushigi said, then started walking down the road.

"Oh!" the woman shouted abruptly. "Come to think of it, I have a scary story, too."

"What is it?"

"So someone I know heard this from one of my friends who lives really far away—apparently, they've seen someone without eyes, a nose, or mouth around town."

"Huh?!" Fushigi ran back over to the woman and stared into her eyes. "Which town?!"

The boy had been quiet the whole ride, so the couple was taken aback by his sudden outburst.

Fushigi, on the other hand, looked entirely serious despite their surprise.

"I've finally found you…"

Fushigi gripped his notebook hard.

Fushigi was walking down the side road.

Then, in an out-of-the-way patch of overgrown grass by the roadside, he saw tire tracks. It looked almost as though the car had driven straight into the weeds.

"So this is it…"

He wondered whether it was the car of the family he'd warned just the other day, but his expression hardly changed.

"Soon. After I collect this one…," Fushigi muttered to himself as he held back his excitement and wandered into the grass alone.

Little Nanoka

Sometimes a very slender woman appears in photos. In America, this apparition is called the Slenderman and is often depicted as male. Supposedly, those who see the slender woman directly are fated to die.

"Okay, smile! I'm gonna take it now!"

On that Sunday afternoon, the sound of a shutter clicked in the park.

Izumi Ichimura snapped a photo of her best friends, Sayuri Niiyama and Rio Komatsu, with her brand-new phone.

Izumi had always wanted her very own phone. She never could convince her parents to buy her one while she was in elementary school, but once she was in middle school and her September birthday rolled around, she finally got one.

"Now all three of us have phones!" Sayuri said to Izumi, and showed off her phone.

"That's so great, Izumi!" Rio smiled and held hers up as well.

"Yeah, I'm so happy! Let's take more pictures!"

Izumi was so excited to be more like her friends that she started another photo shoot.

It was evening on the same day.

Izumi was lounging around on her bed as she scrolled through the pictures she'd taken that afternoon in the park.

In all the photos, whether they were holding up peace signs, smooshing their faces together, or even making funny faces at the camera, they all looked like the best of friends.

I wanna take a whole bunch more tomorrow with them!
Izumi smiled as she started to turn off the screen.
"Huh?"
But right then, one particular photo caught her attention. In it, the three of them were smiling in front of a swing set. The time stamp said it was 1:10 PM. Izumi stood right at the center, while Sayuri was to her right and Rio was on her left. But behind them, she saw a woman she hadn't noticed before.

The woman was standing right next to the swings, but there was something off about her.

Izumi squinted at the photo.

Then she realized the woman was a lot skinnier than should have been possible.

She was also over six and a half feet tall, but she was thin as a twig. Her hair was very long, and she wore black clothes with a black skirt. Her face was blurry, almost as if she had no features.

"Who is that?!"

Izumi tried to remember when she'd taken the photo.

We were on the swings right before we took this one…

Izumi had been taking pictures of herself while on the swings, too.

Then we all got in front of the swings to take a picture together…

She hadn't seen anyone around back then.

Besides, she was certain she would have noticed a slender woman over six feet tall standing right behind her.

Actually, I think I took another photo after this one, too…, she remembered.

She tapped over to the photo, but the woman wasn't in the second one.

"What's going on?!"

Since she'd taken one picture after the other, only ten seconds had passed between them. But the woman wasn't anywhere to be seen in that second shot.

"How could that be…?"

A shudder ran through Izumi.

"What's wrong?"

She suddenly heard a voice from the entrance to her room.

She looked up to see her older brother, Kenji, standing there. Through the gap in the open door, he'd noticed that Izumi was frightened.

"Kenji, look at this!"

Izumi rushed over to him and showed him the picture. Kenji was a whole year older, so she knew she could count on him. He was always there to listen whenever she ran into trouble.

"What's this?" Kenji tilted his head to the side as he looked at the picture.

"There's something weird about this woman, right?"

"Are you sure that's even a person?"

"What?"

Now that he'd mentioned it, she wasn't sure. Whatever was in the photo was very tall and thin, and it also didn't seem to have a face that she could make out. It couldn't have been a person by that description.

"Then what's in the picture?!" Izumi asked, scared out of her wits.

"Dunno. I have no idea..."

"You can't tell, either?!"

Izumi was becoming more and more afraid, but Kenji seemed to have remembered something. His face brightened.

"I've got it! *He* might know!"

"He...?"

"I know somebody who's all about this sorta stuff," Kenji said, and he immediately got in touch with his friend.

Monday, the next day.

It was the anniversary of their school's founding, so they had the day off.

That morning, Kenji led Izumi to a fast-food place in front of a train station. They were meeting someone who might be able to tell them about the woman in the picture.

"I met him recently at the park. He seems to know a ton about urban legends and scary stories."

Kenji liked those kinds of things and had gotten along with the boy right away.

"Urban legends?"

Was the woman in the picture one of those?

Izumi had thought urban legends and spooky stories were just make-believe on the internet and in books.

"Oh, there he is. Him," Kenji said as he stared at the entrance to the restaurant.

Izumi followed his gaze. She saw a boy wearing red clothes and a red hood standing there.

He looked kind of cool.

When he noticed them, he immediately walked over.

"This is Fushigi Senno. He said he's new in town. Fushigi, this is my younger sister, Izumi."

Izumi stood up to greet him, but Fushigi ignored her and looked at Kenji.

"So where's the picture?"

"Huh?"

"I heard you got a picture of a woman without eyes, a nose, or a mouth."

"Oh, right." Kenji signaled Izumi with his eyes to show Fushigi the photo.

"Oh, um. It's this!" Izumi quickly pulled out her phone and showed it to the boy.

He just stared at the picture and didn't reply.

"So, um…," Izumi nervously said, but Fushigi didn't even spare her a glance.

What's with him?

He seemed to not have any interest in Izumi at all. His

focus was entirely on the photo. Just as that thought crossed Izumi's mind, she saw his lips twitch.

"I see... So that's all it was."

He seemed to be muttering to himself—and also seemed put out for some reason.

"What's wrong?" Izumi asked.

"Oh, nothing," Fushigi said. "It just wasn't what I thought it'd be."

"What did you think it was?"

"That's personal." He finally looked away from the picture and sighed softly.

"So does that mean you don't know who the woman in the photo is, either?" Kenji asked, appearing a bit disappointed by Fushigi's reaction.

Fushigi shook his head slightly. "No, I do."

"Then what is she?"

"You have a picture of Little Nanoka."

"Little Nanoka?"

Izumi had never heard that name before. She tilted her head.

Fushigi started to explain who the woman in the picture was.

"She's an urban legend. Basically, a monster that shows up only in photos of kids. Anyone who appears in a picture with Little Nanoka suffers a terrible fate, which is"—Fushigi gave Izumi a solemn look—"that they'll be killed by Little Nanoka within seven days of the picture being taken."

"What?!" Izumi was so shocked that she shouted without meaning to.

"Why would that happen?" Kenji asked Fushigi. He also didn't understand what it all meant.

Fushigi, on the other hand, remained calm as he looked at Izumi.

"You need to be very careful, especially around any reflections."

"Reflections?!" Izumi parroted, but Fushigi didn't elaborate.

He headed toward the exit and left the restaurant without another word.

"Hey! Wait!" Izumi tried to get him to stop, but Fushigi didn't even turn around on his way out. "Kenji, who was that guy?!"

"Yeah… He really didn't seem like he was joking."

Even Kenji was bewildered by the conversation.

After leaving Kenji, Izumi decided to go see Sayuri and Rio, since they were in the photo, too. She didn't believe what Fushigi had said, but she decided she should at least let the other two know.

Fushigi's explanation had been strangely persuasive.

Little Nanoka...

Izumi felt even more frightened by the woman in the picture.

After she heard back from her friends and they met at Sayuri's house, Izumi told the other two about Little Nanoka.

But the two girls just laughed.

"We'll die in seven days? That's obviously a sick joke!"

"Yeah, there's no way!"

Sayuri and Rio were both completely unconvinced.

"I don't want to believe it, either, but there's something weird about this picture!" Izumi said, and she showed her friends the woman again, but neither of them seemed afraid.

"We probably just caught someone behind us at a weird moment. Come to think of it, wasn't there a tall woman walking her dog in the park? Maybe it was her?"

"That's right. I mean, you only just got your phone, Izumi. Maybe you haven't learned how to use the camera properly yet?" Sayuri nodded, agreeing with Rio.

"Well, I did, but..."

Izumi didn't know what else to say.

She remembered she really had taken some pictures by mistake that day when she tapped the button accidentally.

Maybe I got a blurry photo of someone in the background like they're saying, then?

"Fushigi Senno or whatever was probably just making stuff up."

"That's right. You shouldn't worry about it."

She started to believe her friends over Fushigi.

"Yeah, maybe you're right… Actually, I think you two are!"

Izumi was beginning to think that maybe Little Nanoka didn't really exist.

But later on that night…

…Izumi was convinced Fushigi was right.

It was dark. Izumi finished her homework and was about to go to bed when she got a call on her phone. She looked at the screen and saw it said **Sayuri**.

I wonder what happened.

Since it was so odd for Sayuri to call her at a time like this, she picked up the phone.

"Hello?"

"Izumi, I'm sorry for calling so late."

"It's okay. What's wrong?"

"So, um..." Sayuri's voice was shaking for some reason.

Izumi noticed that, and then she heard Sayuri gulp from the other end of the line. Then her friend said slowly:

"So, um...one of my pictures has Little Nanoka in it, too..."

"What?!"

Izumi was so shocked that she almost dropped her phone. "Explain everything!"

"Okay..." Sayuri's voice quivered as she explained.

That evening after Rio and Izumi had returned home, Sayuri had gone to the grocery store for her mom to pick something up. Because the setting sun had looked so nice on top of a hill, she'd taken a photo of herself with the sun in the background.

"I just looked at the picture. Little Nanoka was behind me, too..."

"Send me that picture right now!" Izumi yelled, and Sayuri sent it to her immediately.

Izumi rushed to open it. Just like Sayuri had said, a tall woman thin as a twig and wearing black clothes was standing behind her.

The picture wasn't blurry at all, but she couldn't make out the woman's features.

"It's Little Nanoka…"

So she really did exist.

She was in another picture.

Izumi remembered what Fushigi had said.

"Anyone who appears in a picture with Little Nanoka suffers a terrible fate."

"That terrible fate is being killed by Little Nanoka in seven days after being in a picture with her…"

In that moment, Izumi truly believed the three of them would be killed by Little Nanoka.

It was Tuesday.

Once school was over, she'd invited Sayuri and Rio over to the park, so they were headed there now. She'd asked Kenji to call Fushigi for her in order to ask him more about Little Nanoka.

"Izumi, this is kind of scaring me…," Rio said.

"Me too. I didn't think it'd show up in your picture, too, Sayuri…"

Now Rio was also scared after hearing about what had happened. She'd realized Little Nanoka wasn't just a random person who happened to be caught in their photo.

They met with Kenji at an intersection, then continued toward the park. That was when they spotted Fushigi near the swings. He was staring at something—at a red notebook. When Kenji called out to him, Fushigi carefully put the notebook into his pocket and approached Izumi and the others.

"Did you need something from me?"

Like yesterday, Fushigi was calm.

"Um, please look at this!" Izumi showed him the picture on Sayuri's phone.

"Looks like Little Nanoka," he said.

"That's right. She's in a photo Sayuri took, too!" Izumi said.

"Right," Fushigi murmured as he stared at the picture. "She's closer than in the one you took…"

"What?"

When Fushigi said that, they all looked at Sayuri's photo and Little Nanoka in it.

"Wait, now that you mention it…"

Little Nanoka really was closer compared with their first picture at the park.

"Why is she closer?!"

"She's trying to attack you. That's why," Fushigi said indifferently.

A bad feeling crept over Izumi as she looked at Sayuri and the others, who also appeared more scared than before— they were even starting to tear up.

"Fushigi, is that all true?" asked Kenji, who had been listening the entire time. "How do we stop her?"

He looked serious. Kenji also believed in Little Nanoka now and seemed upset.

"C'mon! If you know how to save them, then tell me! I need to save my little sister!" Kenji firmly said.

"You want to save...your little sister?"

For a second, Fushigi's cold expression shifted. His eyes narrowed, and he seemed to be thinking about something. After staring at Kenji, Fushigi finally said, "There is one way to save them..."

"There is?!"

Izumi and the others perked up.

"Yeah. Little Nanoka only lives in the reflected world."

"The reflected world? You said something about reflections in the fast-food place, too, didn't you?" Izumi said. Fushigi nodded slightly and pointed at a corner of the park, at a bench where a woman was fixing her hair in a mirror.

"That mirror, for example. A mirror reflects a person, right?"

"Yeah..."

"And those pictures you took are also 'reflections' of what you look like, right?"

"Yeah..."

Izumi had no idea what Fushigi was getting at. He seemed to have noticed and said, "In other words, Little Nanoka only exists in the reflected world—in mirrors, pictures, videos, and windows that can reproduce a person's image."

"Huh…?"

That was why she could appear in photos even when they couldn't see her anywhere around.

"If none of you are reflected anywhere in the next seven days, then she'll leave you alone," Fushigi said as he stared at them firmly.

Izumi and the others shared a look.

"So we just need to

make sure we don't have a reflection anywhere for seven days, and we'll be fine?"

"Yeah, that's right."

"In that case, we need to start right now!" Izumi said, and Sayuri and Rio both nodded firmly.

Then they immediately headed home.

It was Wednesday.

Ever since meeting with Fushigi, Izumi had stayed cooped up in her room. Her parents had been worried about her, but Kenji somehow explained things, and they seemed to have come to an understanding. They didn't believe in urban legends, of course, but it was a different matter when she was in danger of being attacked by a sinister-sounding thing of nightmares.

Other than when she went to the bathroom, Izumi stayed in her room.

She removed all the mirrors and even closed the curtains over her windows so that the glass couldn't reflect her. Since even her phone screen could have a reflection, she handed it over to Kenji for safekeeping. Since Sayuri and Rio were doing the same thing in their own homes, Kenji talked with their parents over the phone and relayed messages when they needed to communicate.

After all the girls had gone home the night before, Kenji had gotten more information about Little Nanoka from Fushigi, who told him that exactly seven days after Little Nanoka first appeared in a photo, she would give up and disappear.

Izumi had taken the picture at 1:10 PM on Sunday.

In other words, as long as they weren't reflected anywhere, at exactly the same time the next Sunday afternoon, Izumi and her friends would be fine.

Izumi cowered in bed and prepared to wait it out.

However, things could never be that easy…

It was evening. Kenji carried Izumi's dinner to her room.

"Looks like today went fine," he said.

Kenji had been worried about his sister the entire time.

"Yeah." Izumi was relieved she had such a nice older brother. "Thanks, Kenji."

But when she looked at him, she was shocked as she realized something terrible.

"No!"

The next moment, she leaped back into bed and hid her head under the covers.

"What's wrong, Izumi?!"

Kenji had no idea why she was acting that way.

"You need to go, Kenji!"

"But why?"

Izumi was shivering as she hid.

"Was something reflecting you?!"

Kenji looked himself over, but he wasn't wearing anything reflective at all.

"I don't see anything," he said, but Izumi's arm reached out of the covers and pointed at his face.

"Your eyes! Your eyes have my reflection!"

"Huh?!"

He realized looking at Izumi also created a reflection. And she must have been afraid Little Nanoka was there because of it.

"You need to go, now!"

"Uh, right…"

Even without any mirrors around and with the curtains drawn over the windows, as long as anyone else was in the room with her, Izumi could be reflected in their eyes.

"I'm scared. I'm so scared…"

From that day on, no one went into Izumi's room.

On Thursday and Friday, Izumi continued to stay in her room all alone.

"Izumi, I'm setting your food down."

"Okay…"

After leaving her food on the floor in the hallway, her family would leave, and Izumi would open the door to retrieve it. To stop anyone from coming into her room, she kept her door locked from the inside.

She took her meals all alone and prayed 1:10 PM on Sunday would come as soon as possible. She couldn't talk to anyone, and being alone in her room was nerve-racking.

According to Kenji, Sayuri and Rio were feeling the same. Once they all realized they could be reflected in other people's eyes, they'd also ended up having to stay in their rooms alone.

Please… The seventh day can't come soon enough…, Izumi thought as she ate stew for dinner.

At that moment, her eyes went wide.

"Aah!" Suddenly, Izumi's scream rang throughout the whole entire house.

"What's wrong?!"

Kenji and his parents rushed over to Izumi's room and stopped in front of the door, which opened only for a spoon to come flying out into the hallway in front of their eyes. From the slight gap in the door, they saw Izumi shivering and wrapped in her blanket.

"It's that! It's reflecting me!"

"What?!"

They looked at it—the spoon Izumi had thrown was made of metal. She was afraid it would reflect her, too.

"Hurry and take it away! And close the door, too!" Izumi yelled as she hid her face under the blanket.

Even though her family was still worried about her, they could only say, "All right," and close the door.

It was Saturday.

Izumi became frightened of even taking her meals.

She was so scared of opening the door or talking to her family that she spent the entire time in bed with her head under the covers.

She was even scared to open her own eyes.

Please, please, please, please, please, please, please...

Izumi squeezed her eyes shut under the blanket and prayed for Sunday afternoon to come.

It was Sunday.

It had been raining since morning.

Izumi listened to the pitter-patter of the raindrops as she

stared at the ticking hand of the clock. The wooden needle showed her that it was past eleven AM.

"Just two more hours… Just two more hours and I'll be fine…"

Her eyes followed the second hand as she waited for the time to go by.

Her face was haggard. She hadn't had a decent meal since the day before, and she hadn't slept much, either. She hadn't even talked to her family, and her door had been locked the entire time.

The only thing on Izumi's mind was 1:10 PM.

Time continued to flow, and the afternoon drew nearer.

It was noon, then half past twelve, then 12:55…

"Almost…almost…almost…"

As Izumi watched the second hand, she started smiling without even realizing it.

But right at that moment, she felt something.

Her body couldn't move.

Wh-what's going on?

Izumi tried to lift her hands, but they were like stone, and she couldn't even get her muscles to twitch.

In fact, it wasn't just her hands—her feet and her face were also frozen in place.

Uh, uhhh, uh…

She tried to call for help but couldn't get a sound out.

A-am I paralyzed?! Izumi could only think.

Help, Kenji! Help! She tried to cry out, but she couldn't make a sound.

Why am I paralyzed?!

Izumi tried to will herself to move as if her life depended on it, but she couldn't budge an inch. The only thing she could control was her eyes. She searched desperately with them and somehow tried to turn her head, but the paralysis was too strong.

It was 1:05 PM.

Rattle, rattle!

Suddenly, someone was relentlessly trying to open the door.

It must be Kenji!

She was convinced her brother had come to rescue her, and she turned her eyes toward the door.

Rattle, rattle! Rattle, rattle!

She'd locked herself in, though, so no matter how much he tried the doorknob, it wouldn't open.

What do I do?! Kenji! Kenji!

As Izumi began to regret ever locking the door, she yelled Kenji's name in her mind.

Rattle, rattle! Rattle, rattle! Rattle!

The door abruptly grew quiet. Then, the lock slowly clicked. For some reason, it had unlocked all on its own.

But how? It can't be opened from outside!

Izumi had no idea what was going on. All she could do was open her eyes even wider.

Right at that moment, the door swung open. From the gap created by the ajar door, the hand of a woman emerged.

The nails were long and bright red.

"Heh-heh-heh-heh. Heh-heh-heh-heh."

She heard the shrill sound of a woman's laugh from behind the door.

It was Little Nanoka.

It was the six-and-a-half-foot-tall faceless woman dressed in all black.

Little Nanoka was cackling as she entered the room.

She slipped right up to Izumi.

No! Get away! Izumi tried to scream, but she couldn't make a sound.

She couldn't move in the slightest, either.

"Heh-heh-heh-heh. Heh-heh-heh-heh."

Once Little Nanoka was right in front of Izumi, her faceless head loomed above her.

Then on the monster's blank face, two gargantuan eyes peeled open.

They were red and oh so sinister.

With those terrifying eyes, Little Nanoka ogled Izumi.

"Heh-heh-heh-heh."

Next, her ominous and cavernous mouth parted and began to close in on Izumi.

The inside of her mouth was filled with lots and lots of sharp teeth, like a shark's.

No! Help me! Please! Help!

Little Nanoka continued to cackle away as her large, large mouth loomed ever nearer…

No! No! Noooooo!!!!

Izumi prepared herself for the end…

Riiiiing!

Suddenly, she heard an earsplitting noise.

Izumi whipped up her head and realized her alarm clock was ringing.

"Izumi! Are you okay?!"

Kenji and her parents had run to her room after hearing the sound.

"I-I'm fine," Izumi answered.

At the same time, she realized she could speak again. She could move, too.

"Izumi! Thank goodness! It's the seventh day!"

"What?!"

When she looked at her clock, she saw it was past 1:10 PM. The alarm had rung because Izumi had set it earlier.

"What happened to Little Nanoka, then?!"

Izumi remembered the monster had almost gotten her. She looked all around the room in a panic, but she didn't see any sign of the creature.

"Maybe…it was all a dream?"

Izumi had no idea if what had happened was a nightmare or not.

But when she spotted her doorknob, her stomach lurched. She saw bright-red stains on the knob.

"So it really wasn't a dream, then…"

Izumi's pale face was reflected in the metal doorknob.

Monday, the next day.

Izumi, Sayuri, and Rio headed to school together. The other two had also survived all seven days.

Izumi told them about how Little Nanoka had almost gotten her in the end.

"Was that because Little Nanoka was reflected in the doorknob?" Sayuri suddenly asked Izumi.

"Yeah, I think so…"

But the doorknob had been curved, which warped the reflected world, so Little Nanoka couldn't easily maneuver around. That was how Izumi had survived.

"But we're fine now!"

The seven days had passed, and they could leave their fear of Little Nanoka behind them.

As Sayuri smiled and said that, she pulled out her phone.

"We can start taking pictures again today!"

Izumi and Rio also smiled.

"You're right! Okay, let's take one now."

"Yeah!"

They immediately prepared to snap a pic with Sayuri's phone.

"Are you ready? Give me your best smiles, girls!" Sayuri held her phone out, and the three of them grinned at the camera lens. "Cheese!"

The shutter sound went off…and in that moment—a bloody hand reached out of the screen.

"What?"

The hand grabbed Sayuri's face and dragged her right into the phone.

"Sayuri!"

It had all happened in an instant. Sayuri had disappeared without a trace.

"Sayuri! Sayuri!"

"Izumi, what just happened?!"

"I have no idea. But that hand—it was…"

Its nails were long and bright red from blood.

That had been Little Nanoka's hand.

"Wait, does that mean…?" Izumi suddenly realized something. "Seven days still hadn't passed for Sayuri!"

Little Nanoka had been in Sayuri's picture on Monday evening the week before. In other words, she still needed to wait until that night.

"No…"

Izumi felt a shock run through her as she realized that.

Little Nanoka had gotten what she wanted.

"Heh-heh-heh-heh."

They felt as if they could hear Little Nanoka's shrill laughter from far off…

A few days had passed since then.

A boy was waiting at a bus stop.

That was Fushigi.

He held a bright-red notebook in his hands. It seemed he had collected the mark in that town and was heading off to the next place.

He studied his notebook intently.

Then all of a sudden, an older person lined up behind him peered into Fushigi's face.

"Oh my." The old granny wouldn't stop gawking.

"What?" Fushigi asked, seeming peeved.

"Haven't we met before?" she asked him. "Don't you remember? In that town during your trip. I think you might have been wearing a black hood back then."

"A black hood?!"

"Oh? That wasn't you then? I didn't get a good look at the little child's face, so I was convinced it was you based on your clothes and height…"

Fushigi stared right at the granny. "Which town was that?"

Eventually, the bus arrived, and all the people who had been lined up at the stop boarded.

Only Fushigi showed no sign of getting on. He was looking at his notebook instead. A single beat-up black-and-white photo was sandwiched between the cover and first page. In the photo, Fushigi was smiling beside a girl who looked just like him.

"I'm going to catch you eventually, Himitsu…"

Fushigi murmured to himself, then closed his red note-book and started walking off alone to the town the granny had told him about.

To be continued…

AFTERWORD

You're terrified, but your curiosity gets the better of you anyway—I think that's the true draw of urban legends.

This novel is about six urban legends in six different towns. All of them should be shudder inducing, and they each have something that makes them unique.

First Town: The Wriggler

What makes the wriggler so frightening is that once you witness it, it follows you forever no matter where you go. Even if you only happen to see it by accident, it simply won't stop pursuing you, for reasons unknown. On top of that, if it catches you, something bad will happen. I think that would be a very scary experience.

No one knows what the wriggler actually looks like, why it wriggles, or what makes it follow people. People fear things they don't understand. I think the wriggler represents that fear of the unknown.

* * *

Second Town: The Truth of the Red Crayon

What would you do if you found a hidden room in your house no one knew about? In this story, strange occurrences keep happening in a house someone has just moved into.

When the little heroine is home with their family, the house isn't scary at all, but for some reason, things get spooky when everyone else isn't around. When you wake up in the middle of the night and walk down your hallway alone, have you ever felt scared? That's the kind of terror this story covers.

Third Town: The Bizarre Cat

Urban legends get passed down from one person to another. In this chapter, a certain story is making its way around. And just so you know, even though the cat might look odd, it isn't actually scary. Plenty of urban legends are strange but not scary.

Fourth Town: Love Spells

Anyone would want their crush to like them, and during those times, a love spell will do the trick. But what if there's a frightening secret to the charm?

There's always something alarming hidden behind every urban legend. And even a spell that seems like fun and games at first has something more sinister hiding behind it.

When using love spells, be very careful what you wish for.

Fifth Town: Sugisawa Village

There's an old legend that deep in a certain mountain, there's a creepy hidden village named Sugisawa. Some people have claimed on TV and the internet that they've actually been there.

But no one has any idea where the village actually is.

This story is about the truth of that village. Some places shouldn't be visited just to satisfy your curiosity.

Sixth Town: Little Nanoka

Now, this is the Japanese take on a popular urban legend in America: the Slenderman. Apparently, when the mysterious man appears in photos, you're in for some trouble.

A certain person suddenly encounters an urban legend. This story is about what to do in those situations.

There are many more urban legends around. I'd be so very happy if you read the second volume, too.

May 2015
Midori Sato

Fushigi Senno is visiting your town right at this moment.

When I was about your age, an American TV show called *The Fugitive* used to air every week. It was so popular that people would disappear from the streets whenever it was broadcast. This was because back then you couldn't record anything, so you had to watch it when it was on.

It was the story of a doctor who traveled all over America in search of his wife's killer after being falsely accused of the crime. The doctor would gather leads of the killer's whereabouts and travel from town to town looking for them. Basically, he would travel from place to place as easily as the wind.

I thought it was a pretty cool made-up story when I was watching it, but one day, I was in for a rude awakening. Apparently, the story was based on something that had actually happened. A doctor had been caught and charged as his wife's murderer and claimed he was innocent even while the show was on the air. The incident was well-known in America, but it didn't get around to Japan until *The Fugitive* gained popularity.

Even a story I'd thought was make-believe turned out to be based on a true story all along.

So I've been producing *True Tales of Terror* (*True Tales* for short) for over fifteen years. But in actuality, I initially presented the program as a direct-to-video movie in 1991, so it has a quarter of a century's worth of history behind it. I've spent that long span of time around scary and mysterious stories. I've even traveled all over Japan to take photos for *True Tales* and have visited real spirit spots. That's why I call myself a horror collector, and these experiences seem to be how the protagonist of this book, Fushigi Senno, was created.

Oh? You noticed I said "seem to be" just now? Isn't that weird, considering I'm the one supervising this series? That's because I don't remember exactly how Fushigi Senno came to be.

While I was talking with Midori Sato, who worked on *Urban Legends You're Not Supposed to Know*, and our editor, S, about creating a new work, we settled very easily on making the story about a young boy who goes on a trek all around the nation collecting spooky and mysterious things. It was almost as though we all knew who the boy was. Just like how *The Fugitive* has its own real-life model.

So I can't help but feel like Fushigi Senno is walking through your town right now with his notebook, copying the marks of horror he comes across.

But why is Fushigi going around collecting these things of horror? It's because he has someone he's got to find. Now, who could this mystery person be? Until next volume...

Norio Tsuruta